THE LOST ANGEL

ANGELS & DEMONS
BOOK ONE

LILLIAN MCCOY

EDITED BY
REBECCA JAYCOX

Dedicated to my family, who has always supported me and my writing career.

PROLOGUE

In the beginning, there were two.
Brothers. Twins. The First Ones.
Together, they created the universe.
Atoms, planets, stars, galaxies.
Nothing became everything in an instant.

But that alone did not satisfy them.
From their restlessness, life was born.
Life on Heaven and life on Earth.
Both worlds prospered and grew under their gaze.
But peace did not last.

Demons rose into being—life that should have never been.
Humans fell first, their souls devoured mercilessly.
Brave angels ventured out to slay the beasts.
Despite managing to exterminate them, tragedy followed.

The Great Healer, one of the First Ones, perished at the hands of the Seven Demon Lords.

The Healer's brother searched desperately for the Healer's reincarnation.

He was never found.

ALL THAT WAS LEFT WAS His sword.

A symbol of hope and strength to the angels of Heaven, and a reminder to the lonely God that his other half was missing. Forever.

CHAPTER
ONE

ADRENALINE PUMPED THROUGH HIS VEINS. EVERY SENSATION and emotion boiled inside him as he basked in the power of the gigantic sword in his tan hands. Its staff-like handle and thick guillotine blades alone stole everyone's gaze.

He smirked as he strangled the handle tighter. His emerald eyes looked to the sky.

Angels above him wore the same uniform he did—a white tunic with fiery-red pants. But instead of standing unified, him and the angels above stood in a standoff. A standoff that ended when the army charged towards him.

Feathered wings burst from his back before he rocketed to the sky. Their shouts intensified as he zipped through the air.

He slashed his sword. Two soldiers fell.

Another guard struck, but the green-eyed angel blocked the blow easily. His opponent shoved his sword closer. They each struggled to land the final blow.

The rogue angel danced around his opponent and stabbed him in the back. A horrible sound emerged from the soldier as he gagged on his own blood.

He yanked out the sword, and the winged guard fell to the courtyard below. Drops of gold blood splattered the air.

The crazed angel took a moment to admire the gold blood drenching the blade.

A chuckle escaped from him.

The angels surrounding him gazed at him in horror, but that didn't matter anymore. He couldn't stop smiling. He wouldn't stop.

He shot across the sky. Swords clashed against his, but there was nothing the toothpicks could do. Nothing.

Angel blood rained from the sky. The more shimmering, liquid gold he saw, the louder he laughed. His once cool green eyes shook with madness.

He flipped around. Another angel aimed his palms and blasted a laser toward him.

The green-eyed angel raised his hand, and a shield of light formed in front of him. The white laser fizzled to nothing.

The shield started to enclose his body like a bubble, but there was still an opening behind him.

"DO IT NOW!" a voice echoed across the battlefield.

The angels shot a barrage of lasers. Did they really think their attacks would reach him in time?

He smirked. A smirk too demonic for an angel. He held up his sword and swung. A burst of light flashed from the steel. The lights crashed into each other.

"Get back!" an angel screamed.

Sparks burst off his blade and singed those close by. They shouted angrily, painfully, but he didn't listen to their useless words. They were pathetic, like they always had been.

"You traitor!" a voice cried. "Face us. Like an angel of the Pugnare would."

The rogue angel was quiet: staring through the army around him into an invisible abyss.

Face them like a member of the Pugnare? He grinned and snickered to himself.

The same Pugnare who ignored him whenever he entered the room? The same Pugnare who told him to shut up every time he opened his mouth?

He cackled louder and louder. Each time, the soldiers' scowls deepened. But that only made this moment all that more satisfying.

"You think I'm that stupid?" he asked.

He turned around. The soldier who'd called him a traitor was one of the few who could look into his green, soulless eyes.

"Don't worry," he hissed. "I've always been smarter than you. All of you."

The angel's brows furrowed. The look of anger and disappointment in the soldier's eyes only widened the maddened angel's smile.

Finally. They could see how powerless they were. Ignoring him had been a big mistake. Now, they would pay. All of them.

His eyes widened.

Something was behind him. Something much more powerful.

Before he could gather his breath, the shield shattered.

CHAPTER
TWO

My eyes burst open.

I gasped and coughed. It took a couple tries to clear my throat of whatever clogged it. Thirst crashed into me as I drowsily smacked my lips.

I lifted my head off the wooden desk and groaned. That definitely wasn't the most comfortable sleeping position I'd had.

My hand rubbed my neck, trying to massage my sore muscles. When the dream popped into my head, my body froze.

I had no idea what caused it or why it was the same every single night, but a dreadful feeling was always attached to it.

After a winded sigh, I distracted myself by looking around. What I saw wasn't what I expected.

I didn't see my bedroom or even the kitchen. I was in my shed.

When did I go to my shed?

I sat on my chair in front of my desk. An empty bottle of beer rested on the wood. When my gaze wandered behind it and to the floor, smashed shards of glass from many more bottles scattered across the ground. That explained it.

I pushed the chair out and looked at the door. A sliver of

sunlight shone through. Did I really spend the night out in the shed? What was I doing in here anyway?

I groaned and gave up on coming up with an answer. There was no point dwelling on it. Grabbing my chair, I hoisted myself up.

My head thumped and I winced. After a couple breaths, the head rush faded away.

Hopefully, Todd was at my house. I needed an explanation.

THE SMELL of gas and eggs wafted out of the cabin. A pan on the stove inside sizzled. That was a sure sign Todd was in there. I rarely used that thing.

The smell of gas disgusted me, but Todd loved it. I would've gotten rid of it if he didn't. And he was a good cook, so I couldn't complain. I pushed open my back door, the creaking hinges ringing loudly in my ears.

Todd turned to me with a big smile on his face. "Hey, Charles! Welcome to the land of the living."

His blond hair was neatly combed to the side. His hair always looked clean like that, and he liked to brag whenever I mentioned it out of jealousy. My brown hair was always messy, even after I made an effort to style it.

He wore a gray shirt with suspenders and trousers. He could afford a belt, but he said he liked the style, for whatever stupid reason.

My feet stumbled toward my dining table. Thanks to my many practices with hangovers, I managed to sit down without dying.

"Not going to talk, huh?" Todd teased. Each syllable vibrated in my ear.

I covered my face with my hands. "Not so loud, please..."

Todd chuckled. "Yessir."

I cringed. No matter how hard he tried, Todd could never be quiet. In fact, if he tried hard enough, he could talk to someone in town without a telephone. He'd done it before actually.

"I'm making some eggs for you. I hope that's okay," he said with no intention of listening to my answer.

I dragged my fingers across my face and looked at Todd. He could've become a chef. He used to say that if he ever got drafted, that that was what he would be. And after the Second World War ended, he could've gone to culinary school. Yet he was still here, hanging out with a loser like me.

"What happened last night?" I said, a slight slur to my words.

He snickered. "What happened last night was the best time ever. A mix of casino, beer, and more beer." He pointed the spatula in the air. "Although, if I wasn't friends with the casino owner, we would be in serious trouble."

I sighed. "Thanks for the details..."

"Happy to help."

Whenever I asked Todd what happened the morning after we bashed, he never gave me specifics. It was annoying at first, but I would eventually be unwillingly filled in by the people in town anyway. Just the thought of them screaming at me and waving their arms around gave me chills. Some of them used their fists, too. I rubbed my cheek reflexively.

"Why was I in the shed?" I asked.

"Oh, yeah. You said you wanted to meet someone in there. It was weird. I tried to get you back into your bed, but you wouldn't listen. You even kicked me. So, I was kinda forced to leave you out there."

I did some strange things when I got drunk. Todd had been creeped out more than once. It creeped me out, too, but I eventually tried not to think about it too much. I didn't want to admit that everyone was right and I had a couple screws loose, even though I knew it was a definite possibility.

"Sorry," he added.

"It's okay. It spiced things up."

Todd chuckled.

Somehow, no matter how many drinks he had, Todd never got a hangover. At least, not in the time I knew him. Lucky bastard.

The sizzling of the stove stopped, and Todd came over with one plate of two over-easy eggs. "This should help with that bottle-ache of yours." He put it in front of me along with a fork.

"Thanks," I said while trying to sound cheerful.

Todd smiled. "Of course."

He brought his own plate over and sat down across from me. I dug in while trying to ignore my persistent headache.

CHAPTER

THREE

I stared at myself in the mirror with a rusted frame, examining my muddy brown hair, my short scratchy beard, and my wrinkled clothes.

My hand wrapped tighter on the bottle.

The plan for tonight, per usual, was to throw a bash with Todd at the casino and bar in town. Maybe that wasn't the best idea, though. Ever since I came into town, Todd said his parents kept him on a tighter leash. That sent a clear message as to how they, and everyone else in town, viewed me, and I couldn't blame them after my antics.

"Hey! Charles!" Todd yelled outside.

I walked to the front door and pushed it open.

The sun was already setting. I could've sworn it was still the afternoon. Then again, I should've been used to losing track of time by now. My mind seemed to slip through time and space itself, even without the drinks.

Todd strolled across the open yard. Once he noticed me, he waved and jogged over. He wore a big, goofy smile on his face, like always.

"I see you've already started," Todd said, pointing to the bottle in my hand.

"Yeah, but I'm not pickled yet."

He laughed. "It's probably because your tolerance has been going up."

That was a weird thing to mention out of the blue, but it was a reasonable assumption. "Probably."

He nodded and analyzed me with squinted eyes before throwing his arm over my shoulder. "Let's get Charlie out!" he cheered with a grin.

Charlie was my drunk nickname that Todd came up with. It wasn't a very creative invention, but I appreciated it, nonetheless.

I chuckled. "Hell, yeah."

"'Atta boy."

Todd slapped my back and walked away. I followed him to the tiny casino and bar in town with a persistent feeling of apprehension trailing close behind me.

THE SMALL CASINO buzzed with people. Some yelled at the slot machines. Others bounced with excitement at their apparent wins.

Todd and I leaned onto the bar. The harsh scent of whiskey and beer slammed into my nostrils. I watched the craps table from afar while I waited for my drink. I might've had a go later and I wanted to survey the crowd before I did.

Someone was about to roll—a young lady with a thin scarf. She'd won a couple games already, so the crowd was naturally rooting for someone to beat her.

I overheard their whispers.

"She better not get this."

"Man, if she wins again, I'm gonna be pissed."

She tossed the dice and silence overtook the table. The dealer lowered his head to inspect the die.

The crowd's smiles starkly contrasted the woman's scowl. "You gotta be kiddin' me," she said.

Todd shook his head. "Poor dame... She was doing so well, too."

"She was." I nodded and took a sip of beer.

The next person in the round was a man. His skin had a dark tan. His short beard complemented his jawline and his straight black hair was slicked back in a messy way. He wore a black vest over his long-sleeve, button-up shirt.

"Check out that gasser," Todd teased.

The dealer shifted the dice to him. The man picked them up with a blank face.

"He seems confident, that's for sure," I replied.

He barely shook the dice at all before throwing them. The crowd followed his every move. Their mouths opened wide, but nothing came out. Then the crowd exploded.

"Are you kidding me? He makes a stupid bet like that and wins?" I heard someone complain.

"Did anyone else make the same bet?" another person asked.

"No. He's the only one," a man answered with the color drained from his face.

The man smirked. "I told you guys I'd win." He picked up all the chips he won and stuffed them in a bag. "I'm the last player in this round, right?"

No one answered him. They simply watched him with agape mouths as he walked away.

"Damn," Todd said in awe.

My mouth burst into a goofy smile. "Now that's luck."

～

I stood in front of a pool table. The man from the craps table held the cue stick. He lined it up to the solid one ball.

With practiced precision, he took the shot. The solid one ball banged against the stripped two ball, making it roll down a hole.

My mouth gaped open. He saw me watching and grinned.

"My name's Aaron, by the way," he said. "What's yours?"

A chuckle escaped from me. "Aaron is a weird name."

He lifted his chin. "Well, I think it's nice." He walked around the table towards the striped four ball.

One side of my mouth rose into a half-grin. "The name's Charlie."

Aaron struck and both the striped four and the striped six ball fell into opposite holes. Was this guy even human?

"You should meet my friend Todd," I said. "He's around here somewhere."

I scanned the room, but I couldn't find him anywhere. Where the hell had he gone?

A chilling breeze blew against my back, but I didn't care. I crouched beside the wall outside the casino, staring at the wood and spinning the match in my hand.

"Does he usually do this when he's zozzled?" I heard someone say.

"Sometimes," Todd answered. "He does some wacky antics, but nothing too serious."

Why did his voice sound so weird? It must've been the beer. Or maybe it was my mind playing tricks again.

Silent anger seeped out of me. Todd was right. Even when I didn't admit it out loud, my mind was always scattered. Even when I acted completely normal, my head was never there.

I frantically scratched the match against the wooden wall.

They must've not seen or heard me or else they would've stopped me. This alley was pretty dark, though. Soon, it would be bright with flames.

Someone took a step closer to me.

"Hey, Charlie. Let's get you home," Todd said, his voice light-hearted.

I scratched and scratched the match until... It lit. I threw it on the dry wooden wall before they could stop me.

"Holy shit!" someone shouted.

The fire spread quickly for such a short amount of time. Or maybe hours passed. I couldn't tell. My stare was fixated on the flames.

Someone grabbed me from behind and pulled me to my feet.

"What the hell are you doing?" they yelled.

My gaze remained glued to the fire.

They shook my shoulders. My vision was so blurry I couldn't tell who it was.

"Come on! *Snap out of–*"

The shield shattered. The laser cut toward him.

He smashed into the building below. Dust and debris clouded the air, providing cover and impairing the angel's vision at the same time.

He stood up from the dent the impact had created and squinted to see the outline of a familiar figure floating above him. As the dust cleared, the first thing he saw was Her narrowed blue eyes simmering with rage. Soon, every last speck of debris was blown away and all he saw was Her.

The green-eyed angel mirrored Her scowl. "Eli..."

She wore a blue dress that danced elegantly in the air. Her arms were wrapped in silver armor. Her blond hair glistened in the sunlight.

"You have betrayed Heaven and its kin! For that, you will fall."

"You of all people..." He took a moment to reminisce. The memories they shared together only stung him more. "How dare You talk to me like that."

He picked up the sword. His legs bent into a fighting stance.

"Would you like help, Lady Elisha?" an angel asked.

She raised Her hands into fists. "I must do this on My own. Retreat to safety."

"As You wish."

The green-eyed angel and Lady Elisha stared at one another until everyone flew out of sight. It was a tense, awkward silence, where only anger brewed.

Their muscles tightened.

With both hands firmly on the sword, he pounced.

Lady Elisha blinked. When She opened her eyes, they glowed pure white.

Her appearance suddenly changed. The air around Her turned into a white haze. Her skin darkened along with her now wavy black hair. And her eyes glowed a honey shade of brown.

Instead of acknowledging another stranger from my dreams, she looked directly at me. "Wake up, Charles."

A FLASH of light forced my eyes open. I heaved in shallow breaths. My heart punched my chest.

Why did that woman change? Who were they? Why did they freak me out so much?

No. It wasn't that scary. It was just a strange dream, and there was nothing more to it. All I needed to do was take a couple deep breaths and relax. *Relax.*

"Are you okay?"

I lay in a bed, but not in my bedroom. This room was painted white, and the sheets on this bed were green. And this was way bigger than my bedroom. Technically, my bedroom wasn't even a room, but this was.

I turned to where the voice came from. My face warped as I stared at the man, confused. "Aaron?"

He sat at a bench under a window. "Yeah." He stood, walking to the edge of the bed. "Are you feeling alright?"

I nodded. "Yes. It was just a nightmare." *Exactly*.

He nodded back, but his concern didn't disappear. "Do you remember what happened last night?"

I tried my best to drudge a memory. Everything was blurred with alcohol. All I could see was a blinding light—orange and big.

And I remembered the craps table at the casino where I saw Aaron for the first time. His confident smirk.

My head pounded. I grabbed my head and winced, but it did nothing to stop the pain from hammering into me.

"Are you sure you're okay?" he asked again.

I closed my eyes and breathed. The pounding in my head slowly stopped. "Yeah, I'm fine," I said. "I've got a bottle-ache, is all." I lowered my hand.

Aaron examined me with a growing worry. "Do you remember anything, though?"

"I remember..." All I saw in my mind was that blinding light. "Something about the casino."

He nodded. "You set the casino on fire."

I shot up. "*What?*"

I'd never done anything *that* crazy. Why the hell would I set something on fire?

"Did anyone get hurt? How am I not in the slammer?"

"No. All you did was scorch a wall. Everyone managed to get out," he said. "And Todd paid the bail as soon as you got arrested." He smiled for a moment. "You have good taste in friends."

I looked at the sheet covering my lap, horrified. Todd paid my bail? How much exactly? Hopefully, he didn't make himself broke for my drunk, crazy ass.

And why would I try to burn down the casino? That was the one place that I could pretend that I fit in. And setting it on fire was how I repaid it? I didn't know what I would do if that fire ended up hurting someone.

"Would you like some breakfast?" Aaron asked.

Breakfast. Even if we just met, it couldn't hurt. Maybe it would take my mind off this fear burning in my chest. "If you don't mind."

"Of course, I don't," he said. "My wife might. Which, I must admit, is a nice thought."

"Your wife?"

"Yes. Her name's Heather. Very blunt woman."

My gaze shifted to the floor. "Are you sure she's okay with helping me out? Especially after—"

"Don't worry." He wasn't smiling, but he didn't look judgmental, either. "I was just fooling. I haven't always made the best decisions, either."

His emerald eyes pierced through me. My muscles stiffened.

He looked like... the angel in my dreams. He was an exact replica. The golden blood and the screams from that nightmare echoed louder in my brain. How didn't I see it sooner?

I swallowed my dread.

It was my mind playing tricks on me. It had to be.

WE STOOD in a hallway by the stairs. Before he walked onto the first step, someone yelled from downstairs, "You better come back down or else!" That voice must've belonged to Heather.

He glanced at me with a smirk and I pushed my tension away. *It was just a dream.*

"Or else what?" he yelled back.

"Hmm. This food better not burn. Such quality eggs, too. It would be a shame."

Aaron turned to me with his face being a few shades lighter. "We better skedaddle." He sprinted down the stairs without looking back.

I strolled after him, now regretting my decision to have breakfast here. I didn't want to be rude by changing my mind and leaving, though. After all, my mind was messing with me. My dreams were just nightmares. None of it was real.

Aaron was already in the kitchen when I reached the bottom of the stairs. Their kitchen was huge compared to mine. They had a blue and white tile backsplash around the cabinets and a countertop with white and black marble. The dining table was made with black marble, and the chairs were made with some dark wood.

But what caught my undivided attention was the smell.

Eggs and one other thing I absolutely loved: bacon. The aroma rushed towards me like there was a strong current in the room.

Who I could only assume to be Heather stood at the stove, stirring around the eggs. She hadn't turned to greet us yet.

All I could see was her pink apron and black hair, just as dark as her husband's. Although, her hair wasn't nearly as messy.

"Darling." Aaron grabbed me by the shoulders and pulled me close to him. "This is Charles."

She turned her head but kept moving the scrambled eggs in the pan below her. Her skin was so pale I could see the blue veins running through it, but that didn't make her any less beautiful. In fact, her ivory complexion was perfect with her straight, midnight hair.

Pink was definitely her color.

"So, that's the crazy bastard that set the casino on fire," she said.

I gulped. Of course, she'd say that. I was an arsonist now, and I didn't even know why I did it. God, what was wrong with me?

She smiled as these thoughts flicked through my brain. "About time we met another lunatic." She rolled her eyes. "Normal people are so boring."

Now, I really didn't know what to say.

Heather turned back to the stove. "Please sit down," she said in a friendly voice. "It's not like you're going to help."

Aaron flashed a smile at me before heading to the dining table. I followed him, not knowing what else to do, and sat down on the chair diagonal to him.

I leaned towards Aaron. "She seems nice," I whispered. She was gorgeous, too, but I wouldn't tell him that.

"Don't be deceived," he hissed.

"Aaron!" We both sat up straight before she turned her head. "You talking about me again, you jawsmith?"

Aaron beamed and shrugged. "Nothing worth mentioning."

Heather's gaze turned harsh, but it softened when she looked at me. "Don't listen to him," she said with a wave. "I'm a nice lady." She turned back to the stove as if nothing happened. "How many eggs would you like, Charles? And do you mind if they're scrambled?"

"Two please," I said politely, fearing her wrath. "And no, I don't."

"Good."

She brought over our plates first. The food smelled delicious. Especially the bacon.

I looked at Aaron with awe, and he gave me a knowing nod. "My wife is a great cook," he told me under his breath. "But don't tell her that."

Heather was too busy getting her own plate to hear his praises.

When she sat at the table, I thanked her for the breakfast. She said it was no trouble, but I could only imagine all the trouble they went through getting me here. Hopefully, I at least walked on the way here.

I studied my plate with apprehension. This was... odd. They were being so nice to me, even though they barely knew me. *Something's wrong here.*

"I don't think I've seen you around town before," I mentioned.

"Makes sense," Aaron said with a full mouth. He swallowed. "We moved here about a week ago."

That didn't really clear up anything. I would've at least seen them around if they'd been here for that long.

"Really?" I asked. "Have you guys gone into town at all?"

"Only for quick trips," Heather replied.

I still thought it was strange, but it wasn't any of my business. After all, we had just met, even if they were showing me kindness.

I munched on a couple bites of eggs. Heather really was a good cook. Todd had a new rival in town.

"So." Heather shot me a glance with a friendly smile. "What do you do for work?"

My eyes widened. "Work?"

"Yes," she said. "I asked Todd earlier when he came by to drop you off, but he didn't know. I was just curious."

Strange. Why would that question even come into her head after what I had done?

Wait... what *did* I do for work?

"Uh." I focused my mind harder. I knew I had a job. The image was just a little blurred, like a faded dream. "I'm a bartender."

Yeah. I worked at the casino and bashed there on the nights that I had off. My job was how Todd and I met in the first place.

But how did I even have a job when everyone in town hated me? Maybe it was because the people in the casino were like me. Of course, that was how.

"Really? Where do you barkeep?" Heather asked.

"The casino and bar in town."

She sucked in her bottom lip and looked away. "Hmm," she muttered absentmindedly.

The realization of what she probably thought shocked me. I was definitely going to get fired.

FIVE

The three of us stood at the front door.

I was so relieved that I'd met Aaron at the casino. Him and his wife seemed like good future friends.

"Are you sure you'll be alright getting home?" Heather asked.

"I'm sure," I said. All I had to do was find the main street and follow it up to my cabin. Going uphill would be the hardest part. And I was used to the townsfolk screaming at me anyway. It was fair after the stuff I did.

Aaron took a step closer to me. "How about I come with you?" He leaned into my ear. "We live *kind of* close to the casino owner's house..."

What? Why did they have to take me to a house close to the man whose business I literally set on fire?

Why couldn't Todd take me to his house? Oh, right. Lucas. Todd's brother would've smacked me if he ever saw me in their house. His parents would've, too.

But why didn't they take me to my house? Maybe my house was too far away? But whatever the answer, it didn't matter now.

I sighed. It would've been nice to have someone else around.

Considering how pissed everyone in town probably was, they might've done more than scream this time around. "That would be great, thanks."

Aaron nodded and walked toward the door.

"What about me?" Heather asked.

"Make sure the house doesn't catch on fire." He opened the door.

She scoffed and crossed her arms. "Fine." Her gaze softened after a moment. "I *do* have other chores to do." She uncrossed her arms and grinned. "You two walk safe." She looked at me. "And you can come over anytime, Charles."

I bowed my head. "Thank you, ma'am."

"Aww." She put her hands on her heart and made the cutest puppy face I had ever seen. "You could really learn a thing or two from this man, Aaron."

Aaron was already out of the door. He probably ran out as soon as she started ribbing him.

"Shut up," he said from outside. "I'm polite."

I followed Aaron, making sure to keep my mouth shut.

"If we didn't have Charles over, I'd give you a knuckle sandwich."

He folded his arms over his chest. "Yeah, *right*."

Heather slammed the door in our faces. Or rather, Aaron's face.

"Geez." I let out a sigh of relief. "You two sure like torturing each other."

I followed him down the steps of the porch and onto the side of the dirt road.

"I suppose," he said, shrugging. "We don't actually mean it, though. It's more like jests, if anything."

As we picked up the pace, I took a moment to look around us. We were in a part of a neighborhood I'd never been to. The houses were much bigger here.

"This might sound strange, but that's how we show that we care about each other." He thought for a second. "Well, sometimes."

I flashed a smile before sinking deep in thought. "I wouldn't know. I've never been married."

He grunted. "Lucky you."

I looked at the ground. "Yeah."

I didn't know why, but his words filled me with a sickening anger. The image of that woman with raven hair flickered in my head. Then the emotion left. Maybe it was just a stomachache.

WE FINALLY REACHED the top of the hill. We stood under the oak tree in front of my house that gave us both needed shade.

My cabin was... Cozy was one word to put it. There was nothing wrong or unkept about it. It was just small. Most of the houses downtown weren't that much bigger, though.

My heart spiked. Todd stood at my door. He turned around and waved at us, wearing a huge grin. It was a mystery as to how I hadn't seen him earlier.

I looked at Aaron, who had just noticed him, too. He shrugged in response.

We approached him. Todd's smile never faltered as we did.

"I was wondering when you'd get here," he said. "I wanted to make sure you were better."

Aaron's calm expression morphed into confusion. "You could've gone to my house. You know where it is."

Todd shrugged. "I didn't know if you'd all still be there. Figured it would be easier to wait here."

Huh. I supposed that made sense. It was still strange that he didn't check Aaron's house first though, since Todd lived in town, closer to him.

Aaron's eyes narrowed cynically.

"Thanks for paying for my bail," I said, changing the topic. "Tell me how much it is and I can pay you back."

"No can do," Todd replied with a smile.

I glared at him. He always did this.

"Don't flip your wig. I left the fines for you to take care of."

I grunted. I wanted to pay him back, but the fines would have to do for now. And I still needed some time to process everything on my own. I never imagined I'd start a fire—and at the casino of all places.

"All right." I took a step closer to my door. "Now that I'm home, put an egg in your shoe and beat it."

"Oh, come on." Todd flung his hands up. "What do you even do all day?"

"I'm allowed to have *some* secrets," I lectured.

"Is he always like this?" Aaron asked, nodding at me to answer for Todd's nosiness.

"Yes," Todd answered before I could. "He always spends a couple hours each day to himself. I've been trying to get in on whatever he's working on, but he never lets me."

He was talking about the dream. At least, the time I spent thinking about the dream. I didn't know it was for hours, though.

I didn't want Todd to know anything about it. He blamed my craziness on the alcohol and laughed it off most days, but the dream didn't have anything to do with the alcohol.

"Well, then maybe it's best if you leave him alone," Aaron suggested.

"You are my new favorite person," I blurted out.

"What?" Todd dramatically put his hand on his forehead. "How could I get replaced so easily?"

I waved my hand. "Go away and you'll get your spot back."

He straightened his back and saluted. "Yessir." He swung

around and walked away, humming some random tune to himself. He was such an actor.

All Aaron did was nod before running after him. I watched them go down the hill together and exchange words I couldn't hear.

When they were out of sight, I walked inside, the image of that woman with almond skin playing in the back of my mind. I had quite the imagination.

CHAPTER

SIX

I took a sip of my beer, the crisp, bitter taste calming my nerves. Even though the woman with the wavy, black hair only appeared for a second in the dream, her appearance was the one that stuck with me the most. Past the seriousness in her gaze, there was a hint of desperation in her eyes. Like she wanted me to save her.

Someone knocked on the door. I stood up from the kitchen table and swung it open. It didn't surprise me one bit when I saw Todd.

"Let me guess," I said. "You want to have a bash tonight?"

His cheesy smile faded. "Oh, come on. It was going to be a *surprise.*"

I rubbed the back of my neck awkwardly. Any other time I would've laughed at him and gladly went out, but not after what had happened. "I'm not sure if I want to go anywhere after last night. People could've gotten hurt. Maybe alcohol and me don't mix too well."

His mouth dropped. He stared through me as if I'd offended him somehow.

"Then I'll keep a better eye on you," he said. "Don't make me get caught up in antics alone."

My eyes darted away. Maybe, as long as he didn't let me out of his sight—

"Hello there."

We jumped.

Aaron stood behind Todd with a smile on his face. I hadn't even heard him coming.

"A little warning next time," Todd barked.

Aaron's smile turned awkward. "Sorry. I didn't mean to scare you guys." His attention turned to me. "I just wanted to see if I could spend some time with Charles tonight."

Todd's face went blank. "Oh." He turned to me. "Aren't you getting popular, Charles?"

"I guess I am." I shrugged. "But where exactly are we going to go? I don't think anyone wants me back in the casino." *I* didn't want to go back there, either.

Todd put his hands on his hips. "Oh, don't worry." He winked. "I have the perfect place."

"Okay, then," I said. "Where is it?"

"Oh, *gosh*." He tried to sound like a woman, but he actually sounded like he breathed in helium. "I'm allowed to have *some* secrets."

I laughed at his weird impression of me. Why did I sound like a dame to him?

"Um, are *you* okay with going wherever Todd wants us to?" I asked Aaron, only half-joking.

"Of course." He jokingly raised a brow. "Nothing fishy about that at all."

I didn't want to do anymore crazy stunts, but maybe if another person was around other than Todd, then we could relax. Besides, Todd was only trying to cheer me up.

"All right." Todd danced with excitement. "Let's meet at the edge of town at sunset."

A BRIGHT CACOPHONY of colors simmered in the sky as the sun set lower and lower. I clutched the bottle in my hand tighter and looked around. Even though I was at the edge of town, there wasn't a single soul in sight. I was somewhat grateful for that.

I grumbled. "Where the hell are they?"

"I was wondering the same thing."

I whipped around. Aaron greeted me with another awkward smile. I placed my hand on my chest to steady my beating heart. My poor heart.

"How long have you been there?"

He shrugged. "Just got here."

"Oh," I said. "Okay."

I turned away, slightly embarrassed that he'd scared me, and raised my bottle for a sip. I needed to get rid of this awkwardness somehow. Aaron snatched my wrist before anything poured into my mouth. I glared at him in confusion.

"Maybe we should wait until Todd comes before we drink." His face was stern. Serious. *Angry.*

My brows curled. "Why?"

"Just trust me on this one."

Trust him on *what?* We were literally meeting up to drink, and I brought alcohol. What did he expect would happen?

My hand squirmed in his grip, and I parted my lips. Maybe some would spill into my mouth if I twisted hard enough.

Aaron yanked the bottle from my hand and slammed it onto the ground. The glass shattered. The beer spattered on the dirt.

"What the hell?" I screamed.

"Yeah."

We turned our heads to the new voice. Todd stood a couple yards away with his hands casually in his pockets.

"Charlie just wants to have some fun, right?"

"*Yes!*" I thanked Todd in my head for arriving. "The point of tonight is to get wasted. Harmless fun."

The flames on the casino appeared in my mind. That wasn't harmless. Why was I shrugging that off so easily?

That doesn't matter. As long as Todd kept a close eye on me, everything would be fine.

Aaron's expression morphed from shocked to concerned in a split second. Then he regarded me with pity. Sadness, even.

Todd walked toward us. "That's right. Glad we're on the same page." He pointed his chin toward me.

But Aaron scowled as soon as Todd opened his mouth. "Have you been doing this *every* night? Making him drunk?"

I didn't know what to say. Aaron acted like we were close friends after only knowing each other for a couple days. What was happening? What was going on?

Todd shrugged. "We're just having fun." He tilted his head. "But you aren't here for fun, are you?" Todd stopped walking, even though he was still a good distance away.

"What are you talking about?" I asked.

Todd smirked. "He's an undercover cop, aren't you?"

"*What?* No, I'm not," Aaron shouted, anger glinting in his eyes. "I'm concerned about you. Drinking every night. It *can't* be good. Charles set a fucking casino on fire!"

"That's exactly what someone on the beat would say."

Aaron stumbled over his words. "*A cop* would say that he's concerned for his friends' safety? *A cop* would offer his house as a place to stay because it's closer to the casino, so Charles didn't have to walk so far after he set it on *fire*? *A cop* would do all that?"

"Why are you getting so defensive, Aaron?" Todd's voice sounded different than usual. Arrogant. "If you aren't the fuzz, there's no need to flip your lid."

But Todd had good points. The entire town would pounce at the chance to get me locked up. Maybe they hired someone from the outside. Someone to go undercover.

"*Yeah...*" I backed away from Aaron, who seemed crazier by the minute. "Todd has a point there." I stopped beside Todd where it was safest.

Aaron frowned in disappointment. He reached out with his hands. "Come on, Charles. You can trust me. I'm *not* a cop." His green eyes filled with desperation.

But maybe I deserved to be in jail.

"I've only known you for two days. We can't trust you *one bit*," I said, ignoring the thought that popped into my head.

Aaron's hands dropped to his sides in defeat.

Todd glanced at me before he spoke with a smirk. "That's right." He stepped forward. "We can't trust you one bit."

Aaron clenched his jaw. "You *corrupted him.*" His voice sounded like a wolf. A growling, furious wolf.

"I don't know what you're talking about," Todd said with a toss of his head.

"You know *exactly* what I'm talking about."

Nervous laughter escaped me. "Todd corrupted me? What are you rambling about?"

Aaron put his hand out and pleaded with me. "Charles, listen to me and get away from him."

Todd swung his arm out in front of me. "Like he would walk up to a cop who deceived him."

"Listen, Charles." Aaron's pleads only became louder. "You know this isn't right."

The woman's light brown eyes flashed in my mind. "What the hell are you talking about?"

Aaron froze. He slowly leaned back, as if a realization hit him.

I never should've trusted him. I should've known that the town was plotting against me. Todd was the only person here I could trust.

But I should be in jail. I set a building on fire. I set a *fucking* building on fire and I didn't even know why.

Aaron bowed his head. "I was hoping I didn't have to resort to this." His fists tightened. "But now I have no choice." Aaron reached inside his vest and pulled out a pistol.

My lungs tightened. "What are you doing?"

"Freeing you." He pointed the pistol at Todd.

My heart rocketed inside me. I slid in front of Todd before Aaron placed his finger on the trigger. I wouldn't let my best friend be killed.

Aaron's expression faltered, but only for a second. "Move out of the way."

"No." Maybe I could reason with him. "If you are a cop, there's no reason to shoot him. Just take me to jail." Maybe then my episodes would be under control, too.

His head rattled. "I'm not a fucking cop." He slid his finger away from the trigger. "I'm trying to help you."

"By shooting my best friend?"

"That *snake* is not your friend."

"And *you* are?"

He lowered the gun slightly. His determined expression showed cracks. Was it working?

Aaron gritted his teeth and aimed the gun again. Of course, it wasn't.

Todd placed his hands on my shoulders.

Aaron gripped the gun harder. "Get your hands off of him," he ordered with bared teeth.

I glanced back at Todd. Maybe he was scared. I'd never seen him scared, but tonight called for an exception.

But he didn't look afraid. In fact, he was grinning. For the first time ever, I was creeped out by that smile.

"I'm sorry that you had to find out like this," Todd soothed.

My skin crawled. "Find out what?"

He grabbed me and swung out a sword. A real sword. Where the hell did that come from?

The sword hovered above my throat. The cold, sharp metal kissed my neck. Todd's arms suffocated me.

"Todd, what are you doing?" I huffed between quick, shallow breaths.

He didn't answer me. "Put down the gun," Todd commanded.

Aaron's scowl deepened. "Why should I?"

"This sword was made and blessed by Lord Anacora himself. One swipe across his throat and he's dead."

My heart stopped for a moment. *Dead.*

No. Todd was bluffing. He would never hurt me. As soon as Aaron stopped, this nightmare would be over. Todd would let me go.

But why did he go to this extreme? Even accidentally, Todd could kill me with one stroke. He wasn't bluffing, but he had to be. He was my friend.

And what did he mean by blessed? Who was Lord Anacora?

Wind blasted my face. Aaron disappeared. Then the click of a gun cocked behind me, behind us.

"You're not the only one with a blessed weapon," Aaron said.

He was fast. Inhumanly fast.

Todd scoffed. "Lady Elisha was wrong to place her trust in someone like you."

Elisha? That was one of the angels in the dream. It couldn't be. I was hearing things. My mind was messing with me again.

"You don't have the *right* to say her name," Aaron said.

"Oh?" Todd taunted. "And *you* do?"

"What the hell are you guys talking about?" I tried my best to escape from his grip, but I only managed something close to flinches. "Let go of me, Todd."

My neck stung. I gazed down. Drops of blood trickled down my neck as he pushed the blade in slightly. My blood.

He whispered into my ear, "I suggest that you don't move or speak until I tell you to."

I stiffened, trying to stop myself from shaking. The blade only needed to go a little deeper. He only needed one clean swipe and I would be dead.

Todd was my friend.

Damn it. Why was I still thinking that? He was going to kill me.

Aaron grunted. "You're pretty cocky for having a gun against your head."

Todd laughed. "You're not going to kill me, Sarhiel."

Sarhiel?

There was a long moment of silence between us. I scanned the area as much as I could, but there was no one around.

I could've died right now, and no one would've been around to witness it. No one would even care.

"You're right," Aaron conceded.

Something fell onto the ground.

"*Finally.*" Todd released some pressure off my neck, but he didn't let go of me. "You made the right choice for—"

A loud bang rang in my ears. The sword dropped in front of me. After a millisecond that dragged into what felt like centuries, Todd released me and another loud thump followed.

I recognized that sound. I hoped with every fiber of my being that I was wrong, that I was inside another nightmare. My feet turned me around on their own. Todd's body lay flat on the dirt. Blood soaked through his shirt.

My knees hit the ground. I was right. It was the sound of a gunshot.

The life in Todd's eyes faded. He gasped before he stopped breathing. Forever.

I let out a high-pitched, horrified scream. My best friend was dead right in front of me, and my neck still stung from Todd pressing that sword against it. Nothing made sense anymore.

"Where were you?" Aaron asked.

"Sorry," a woman said.

Heather stood a fair distance away with a rifle in her hands. "I had to keep my distance so he wouldn't notice me."

She'd shot him.

Aaron locked eyes with me. I scooted away from him as fast as I could. "Stay away from me."

"Charles, I can explain." He walked toward me.

"*Stay away!*"

He stopped, concern creasing his face.

He was a psychopath. A maniac. Both of them were.

My arms and legs trembled with fear. "I can't believe I stayed at your house."

I glanced at Heather. Her brows dug into her nose. "I can't believe I thought you were a good cook."

Aaron stuck his hand out. "He was *threatening* you."

"You didn't have to *kill* him."

His eyes were calm, unaffected. He didn't regret killing Todd at all.

Todd was dead. Todd tried to kill me. Aaron saved me. Aaron helped murder someone right in front of me. My thoughts were a maelstrom, swirling with contradictions.

I forced myself to stand. "Now, I know." My breathing was heavy. "You definitely *aren't* a cop."

Heather spoke up. "But Charles, he wasn't—"

"No." I sprinted away. "Stay away from me."

Heather appeared in front of me. How could she run so fast?

"I'm sorry, but we can't do that."

"Get away—"

Before I could react, the edge of Heather's palm smashed into my neck. The familiar blackness from passing out closed in.

"...from *me*..."

I fell deep into the abyss.

CHAPTER
SEVEN

An infinite expansion of darkness surrounded me. *I searched for just a little light. Just one other person.*

"Is anyone here?"

No answer.

"Hey! Someone, help me," I cried out. "Please."

I stopped and scanned the room, if I could call this place a room. Nothing was there. No matter how far or fast I ran, nothing would change.

I was alone.

My fingers stoked through my sweaty hair.

Was this how I was going to die? The thought alone gave me goosebumps. I rubbed my arms in comfort.

Then again, was my life really worth living? Getting drunk each night, relying on someone at least five years younger than me. There was... nothing there.

Someone moaned behind me. I turned around.

Todd's familiar face stared back at me. He lay on his stomach. Blood spattered the ground as he heaved desperately.

My lungs strangled me.

I wanted to move, to do something, to help. But I was frozen. All I did was tremble.

Todd crawled closer and closer. His eyes clung stubbornly to life. His hands were covered in scarlet-red blood. So much blood.

"Why..." he croaked. "Why didn't you help me?"

He stopped at my feet and weakly grabbed the edge of my pants. "I thought..." He pulled himself up, movements sluggish, and looked at me. His brown eyes were grayer than I remembered.

"I thought... we were friends..."

Tears gushed from my eyes. I thought they'd killed him, but he was still alive. There was a chance. We could escape together.

He's my friend.

I grinned and choked back the tears, but that didn't stop them from coming. "We are friends."

I bowed down and reached out my hand. We had to get out of here. There was no telling what Aaron and Heather would do next.

His brown eyes sparkled with hope. He reached for my hand with a tiny smile. Then his eyes widened, and he made a gurgling sound, something between a cough or a gasp. A huge sword stabbed through his back.

No.

His hand dropped to the floor.

He was dead. Todd was dead.

I stared at his killer. Menacing green eyes glared back at me. Dark shadows cast over his face.

"That snake is not your friend."

MY EYES JERKED OPEN. Heavy breaths accompanied my hammering heart.

Calm down. It was a dream. It wasn't real. I gradually breathed in deeper and slower, but my heart still throbbed in my chest.

I lay on a bed. I jerked my arms and legs, but I couldn't get up. I was tied down.

A thump came from the hall. Aaron stood in the doorway, looking right at me.

Oh God. Not all of it was a dream. Aaron and Heather really did kill Todd. And his face didn't show a hint of remorse or guilt. In fact, he looked perfectly calm.

There was nowhere to go. Nowhere to run.

"I can explain this." He spoke smoothly, as if this situation was normal.

Anger took over my body, even with my overwhelming fear. "You killed Todd. There's nothing else *to* explain."

He didn't react. I wanted to slap him, punch him, to do something. Todd *didn't* deserve to die. But wasn't Todd going to kill me? Why did I persist on defending him?

"You're a backstabber and a murderer," I said, even after contradicting myself in my mind.

He took a step closer. "He was trying to kill you. I did what I had to."

My jaw dropped. The feeling of Todd's blade digging into my throat haunted me.

He was my friend.

My eyes narrowed. "I still don't trust you."

He shrugged. "That's reasonable. But all I ask is that you hear me out."

"It's not like I have a choice."

He stalked closer to me. His footsteps reminded me of a ticking clock. Each second he got closer, my heart beat faster.

He towered over me for a long moment before he sat down in a chair next to me.

"Todd was an enemy agent. He was from the Cloud, an organization that Anacora founded to keep a closer eye on fallen angels. He never intended on being your friend. He only wanted to manipulate you."

What? Todd wouldn't do that to me. He was about to let me go when Aaron ruined it all. *He ruined everything.* And why did Aaron randomly bring up fallen angels? Was he a part of some cult?

"Anacora?"

He scoffed. "Yes. The so-called *Lord.*"

Todd had said that name when he put his sword against my throat.

I swallowed. He was going to kill me, wasn't he? Todd was really going to slit my throat. But maybe I was just being paranoid. Todd was just bluffing. *He was my friend.*

Aaron noticed my expression. "What is it?"

My eyes darted away from him. I couldn't look at him. Not right now.

My mind was scrambled again. I'd felt this many times before. Thoughts switching around, memories changing constantly. My soul was always tearing itself apart. That was why the beer was so comforting.

Still, I tried my best to describe what I felt to him. "I know that Todd threatened me and that he could have killed me. But my heart is still insistent on taking his side. I... I can't..."

His gaze hardened. "He has messed with your mind. That was his mission."

The shock forced my eyes to look at him. "What are you talking about?"

This was how my mind always was. Even when I was a kid before I moved into that town, I never felt completely in the present. This was how I was born.

And why was I talking to him casually like this anyway? He had me strapped to a bed for fuck's sake.

Aaron braided his fingers together. "Do you believe in angels?"

"No." Most people in town were Christians, but I refused to believe a loving being could make a messed up world like this.

All Aaron did was smirk. "Really?"

I didn't know what to say.

He stood up. His glare intensified, brewing with anger.

I feared the worst. Torture? Death? There was no telling what he would do.

Aaron looked down at his suit and started unbuttoning his blazer. Wait. What was happening?

He took off his blazer and his undershirt. The buttons came off slowly, methodically, but I'd seen this before. Right before a fight started. And I couldn't move to stop him. I was going to take a beating and there was nothing I could do about it.

My breaths shook. I tried to force them down, but I ended up just making them louder.

Aaron slowly turned around. My jaw dropped at what I saw.

On his back were two mangled scars. Except, they weren't just two big scars. Each one was made up of smaller gnarled scars stitched into his skin. There must've been hundreds, or thousands, of cuts.

"What..." I breathed in shakily. "What happened?"

His hand reached over his shoulder and grazed one of his scars. "Lady Elisha gave them to me." He didn't speak with anger like I expected from getting such horrific scars. Only sadness and regret, and something else I couldn't quite grasp.

There was that name again. Elisha.

My vision glided down to the floor. "The angel in the blue dress," I thought out loud.

Aaron whipped his head over his shoulder. Just like at his house, his resemblance to the angel in the dream was unmistakable.

I shook my head. "This can't be real."

His teeth showed through his grin. "You received my memories." The smile faded with a darkened gaze. "That's good." His tone definitely didn't match his words.

"Your memories?"

"Yes." He picked up his suit and stood. "And soon, you'll get yours back as well."

Aaron slid his arms into the sleeves of his shirt. Nothing in his movements or his expressions told me that this wasn't some elaborate lie or a panic-and-a-half. He was serious.

"You're crazy." It had to be true. *None of this is real.*

He slid his blazer back on. "I know." He smirked teasingly. The resemblance to the angel in my dreams couldn't be ignored anymore.

I blinked over and over, but the sight didn't change. It couldn't be a coincidence. But angels didn't exist.

Aaron headed back to the hallway.

"Where are you going?"

He didn't answer me or look back. He left and I was alone.

Another set of footsteps walked toward me, and a face peeked inside the room. Heather.

"Hello, Charles."

Wrath exploded inside of me. She was the one who'd *really* killed Todd. My best friend was dead because of her.

"Get away from me!" I shouted with more confidence than I felt.

She ignored me and made her way to the bed. I bared my teeth like a rabid dog. One more step and I would bite her hand off.

Wait, what? Why would I even think about doing that? I needed more answers. I wanted them to tell me everything, but all I did was shake furiously. My muscles spasmed on their own without my conscious command.

As soon as I realized that, a switch flipped inside me. I moved and growled and spoke threats, but it wasn't *me*. Not really.

I focused and tried to get myself to stop, but nothing worked.

Nausea and fear overcame me, starkly contrasting the fuming rage I projected. What was happening?

"At least he knows a threat when he sees it. That bastard should've never let me fall."

I tugged at the restraints. "Get away from me. I'm warning—"

She slapped her hand onto my head. The void consumed me yet again before I could stop it.

"*You...*"

EIGHT

Streams of puffy clouds dotted the sky. Their edges sparkled like feathers against the sun.

I breathed in the fresh air. This field was the perfect place to watch the clouds. Trees surrounded me and isolated me from the rest of the world.

"What are you doing?"

The voice sounded like a girl's, but I didn't bother to look.

"Looking at the clouds," I answered matter-of-factly.

"Why?"

"The clouds are so beautiful, but no one bothers to look at them. They're too busy or they're distracted by all the other things, so I'm doing it for them."

"But you've been doing it for hours," she said.

I turned toward her, her words surprising me. She wore a white dress that flowed down to her ankles. The dress popped against her warm chestnut skin and raven hair.

A breeze passed. The way her dress and her hair danced in the wind made her look so pretty. Even more pretty than Lady Elisha Herself.

"Have you been watching me?"

Red splashed her cheeks. "Um…" She looked down at the grass between her toes. "Sorry. I didn't mean to. I was just—"

"Don't worry. I'm not mad."

Her head snapped towards me.

I offered her a smile.

Her face scrunched. "You're weird."

"A lot of people say that to me. I take it as a compliment." At least, I tried to.

Her blush rushed back to her cheeks before her eyes darted to the ground again. She fidgeted with her dress. What was she so nervous about?

She spoke again. "Can I—"

"Can you what?"

She stopped fidgeting, but she wouldn't meet my eyes. Whatever she wanted to say had to be scary, so I waited patiently.

"Can I watch the clouds with you?"

I sighed with relief. I thought she had something bad to say.

"Of course, you can."

She tried to hide her smile, but she wasn't very good at it. She couldn't even hide her blush.

I didn't really care why she was so nervous. I just wanted to know what she did to make herself look so pretty.

She walked over and lay down next to me. When she seemed satisfied, I gazed back up at the sky.

One cloud resembled a swan. I heard of their grace and poise on Earth. I also heard swans were inspired from angels. Where had I heard that again?

"What's your name?" she asked.

"Caleb."

"I'm Naomi."

I couldn't help myself. I peeked at her again.

She was lying on her side towards me. She wasn't watching the clouds at all. Had she been like this the whole time? Her nerves spread to me at the thought.

But her eyes. Her eyes were so beautiful. They were a light brown, the color of honey or sand. So bright and so cheerful. They reminded me of how the sun met the lake and made it glisten.

Her brows curled. "What? What is it?"

"Your eyes." I paused. "They're really pretty."

She blushed again, but instead of looking away, she kept staring right back at me.

I sat among a sea of people. Everyone rested on their knees and looked to the stage ahead.

Lady Elisha perched on the stage on a silky blue pad. Instead of facing us, She looked to the right. Her glistening blonde hair complimented Her ceremonial white dress.

Naomi lay on another pad in front of Her. She wore a white dress as well, like the one I'd met her in. She had grown so much since then.

I was lucky to have met her and to have been her friend. I was lucky to be at her Second Blessing Ceremony.

"Naomi." Lady Elisha's voice was soft, but loud enough for everyone to hear. "You have proven yourself to be a worthy and kind angel. Not just to Me and the Gods before, but to your family and friends as well."

She put Her thumb in the bowl in front of Her and reached to Naomi's forehead.

"Therefore, by the power invested in all of us." She traced Her thumb on her head before lowering Her hand. "I give you your Second Blessing."

Lady Elisha bowed to the floor first. Then Naomi. The crowd bowed as well, including me.

"Long live Naomi," we said in unison.

I wanted to scream those words, but it wouldn't have been proper. And Naomi would tease me for the rest of my life. Then again, that wouldn't be so bad.

~

I STOOD IN THE FIELD. The flowers around me were in full bloom—pink, purple, violet, white. The stage was set perfectly.

A shadow cast over me. I looked to the sky and saw a figure flying above me. She brimmed with happiness as she flew towards me.

I grinned and spread my arms out. I caught her and spun her around like a child.

We laughed together. When I stopped spinning, I kept my hands on her shoulders. Her wings had long disappeared by then.

"I'm so happy for you," I said.

I backed off after I noticed some pink on her cheeks.

The mark God made on her head was still there—a red crest with a dot beside it.

Today was her one-hundredth birthday, the day of her Second Blessing. The symbol showed that to all of Heaven's angels. It was something to be proud of.

"Thanks," she said. "Was it as entertaining as yours?"

I waved dramatically. "Mine wasn't even close."

I had my Second Blessing a year earlier. That meant that both of us were adults now.

She took a step closer to me. "I wouldn't say that."

I shook my head. Sometimes, I didn't know what to say to her. When we'd first met, she was so shy. What a facade that was.

I glanced at a tree and walked toward it. "Come on." I waved for her to follow.

She did. "What is it?"

I stopped beside a tree. She stared at me like I was crazy. Pretending to be discreet, I reached behind the tree and grabbed her present. Excitement sparked in her eyes.

I held it behind my back, teasing her.

"Did you make me something?" she asked.

I smiled. "What do you think?"

She bobbed her head around to try to sneak a peek. I hid it the best I could.

She jumped up. "Come on. Show me!"

"I don't know. It's not often that I'm the one who teases you."

She gave me a warning glare before lunging. I dodged her easily. She stumbled and regained her balance on a tree.

"Caleb!"

I laughed before showing her what I'd made. She gasped.

It was a crown made from flowers. I used the pink, purple, and white flowers spread across the field. Of course, I used mostly purple, her favorite color.

I walked closer and placed it gently on her head. She didn't move a single inch as I did.

Her fingers grazed the petals of her crown. "You made this?"

I nodded.

"It's amazing."

She played with the flowers on her head with a smile. How did she get so beautiful just by smiling? Maybe it was a superpower.

Her brown eyes glanced at me. "What is it?"

Even in the shade of the trees, her eyes sparkled. Every part of her was shining today. Her white dress, her dark hair, and the red mark on her head.

The longer I stared, the more bewildered she became. She lowered her hands to her sides. Her bottom lip dropped slightly, barely enough for me to notice.

I took a step closer. "You are the most beautiful..." And another. "The most elegant angel I have ever met."

She giggled. "And you are the strangest I have ever met."

I chuckled softly as I moved closer and wrapped my arms around her waist. She blushed like when we were kids.

"Those eyes..." I brushed a wavy strand of hair out of her face. "...are the prettiest eyes I have ever seen."

Her head tilted to the side. "They aren't that special."

That wasn't true. Every time I looked into her eyes, I was weightless, floating in the air with her, and nothing else mattered. All that did was me, and her.

I touched her cheek. Her skin was so soft. Her lips were so close. Maybe, just maybe, I could feel her lips, too.

"I have been waiting to ask you for so long," I confessed, glancing anxiously at her lips.

My heart thumped loudly. Not with fear, but with excitement. Her heartbeat thundered through her own chest loud enough for me to feel. Was she nervous, too?

"Will you be my soulmate?" I asked.

Her eyes welled up with tears. But at the same time, she smiled. Was that a good sign?

"Caleb." She spoke to me like I was an idiot for even asking. "We already are soulmates."

Wait. She said yes? She said yes!

Happiness burst out of me. I didn't know whether to laugh or cry. But I had to do something. Anything.

I kissed her.

She startled in surprise, but then she leaned in closer. I closed my eyes to savor it all. Her soft lips smoothly glided across my own. Her breath tasted like fresh strawberries. The rest of her smelled like grass.

This was pure bliss.

CHAPTER
NINE

A TEAR TRAILED DOWN MY CHEEK.

"Naomi."

This couldn't be real. This had to be a dream—a nightmare to be separated from her.

The woman from my dream was Naomi. The desire to see her again and hold her in my arms crashed into me in relentless waves. But where would I look? I didn't even know if she was still...

Heather slowly took her hand off my forehead before I could finish my thought. Hell, I didn't want to finish it.

I was in the exact same place. Tied to a bed with one of my kidnappers.

"What did you do to me?" I asked.

Her expression cracked. "I—"

A loud boom shook the room violently. Heather smacked into the wall. My heart pounded in my chest. The explosion set Heather into action. She dived for my restraints and untied me.

"What's happening?" I demanded, frightened.

Another explosion.

Heather crashed onto me. She got back up unfazed and continued undoing my restraints. My heart wouldn't slow down.

"Ravens. They're attacking."

"Ravens?"

She finally got the restraints off of me. Before I could stand, she picked me up and carried me. She did it so easily, too.

"What are you—"

"No time for questions!"

She was so confident, and yet, I sensed a trail of fear in her voice. She sprinted into the hallway. So many questions whizzed past me, but I couldn't ask any of them. My mouth wouldn't open.

Naomi.

She was the reason purple was my favorite color. She was the reason I liked when someone teased me. She was the reason I never even thought about loving somebody else.

But was any of that really real? Was *she* real?

Another explosion.

The shaking didn't faze me. Only her face. I became numb with an overwhelming emotion. Walls surrounded me, but it felt like I was in an abyss, floating aimlessly.

"Naomi..." I couldn't even recognize my own voice. It sounded like death. Like I was dying.

Heather looked down at me. Her eyes were a deep brown, almost jet-black, like the bottomless abyss I found myself in. Before I could process anything—like the fact that someone was carrying me and Naomi was out there somewhere and I was here all alone—she threw me onto a chair in a different room.

She ordered something that I couldn't catch and ran back out.

I couldn't stop her from running away. I couldn't do anything. Pulling my knees to my chest with shaky hands, I wrapped my arms around them.

I'd been kidnapped, my best friend of three years had been murdered, and I didn't know who I was anymore. The only reassuring thing was the girl with the sandy brown eyes, and I wasn't even sure if *she* was real.

My palms dug into my forehead.

Along with this intense confusion, there was something else. An emotion that exploded inside me and burned with an undeniable conviction. Fear. But it was different somehow. Like it came from a different person entirely. But that didn't make any sense.

Tears stained my shirt before I realized I was crying. I wiped my eyes, but it was useless. The tears didn't stop flowing.

"Where are you?" I cried as a feeling of helplessness crashed over me.

CHAPTER
TEN

THE MINUTES DRAGGED INTO HOURS. I TRIED GUESSING HOW long I had been left alone, but it was pointless. Maybe an entire day passed, or maybe it had only been an hour. My mind could never process time before, but the shock I'd absorbed only amplified that.

I stared at the floor in a trance, eyes puffy from my earlier wails. After a while, my emotions had slid back into the dark holes they'd escaped from.

Instead of the storm of emotions I endured earlier, my thoughts remained scattered and fragmented. All I could think about was her: her teasing smile, her shiny brown eyes, and her lips painted with strawberries.

Those memories were bittersweet. I wasn't with her anymore. I didn't even know who *I* was. No one gave me the answers I needed, and I wasn't even sure if I'd accept them.

Todd was my friend.

Stop it. He was never my friend. What kind of a friend would put a sword to their friend's throat?

I sank deeper into my chair.

We lay down on her house's cobblestone roof. The stars above shimmered and danced.

My arm wrapped around her waist. Naomi's face nuzzled into my neck.

I smiled and closed my eyes. The sight of the stars didn't satisfy me nearly as much as her touch.

I squeezed my arm and I was back.

Why did she keep popping up? My mind was untangling itself just like it had done so many times before. Each time she bombarded me, I teemed with frustration. My thoughts were spiraling out of control and there was nothing I could do to stop it.

But another part of me wasn't upset at all. Another part of me wanted my mind to stay like that. At least then, I'd be with her.

Footsteps marched toward me. My heart jumped as I shot out of the chair.

It had to be Aaron and Heather. But they were under attack. I had no idea if they were defeated, and now their enemies were inside here, wherever here was.

They stopped at the door and it swung open.

I covered my mouth with my trembling hands. Blood splattered on Aaron and Heather's mangled clothes. Their arms wrapped around each other for support.

Heather was much worse than Aaron. While Aaron was bruised and battered, Heather was completely bathed in blood.

"What—" I took in a quaking breath. "What happened?"

Aaron's gaze hardened. "Heather's wounded. Bad."

That part was obvious, but some of her injuries looked like

they came from bullets while the gashes along her arms definitely came from a blade.

I wanted to move, but my feet wouldn't budge. I had to help them, right? They saved me from that place, whatever the hell that place was.

Todd was my best friend and they killed him.

Shut up.

Heather's eyes lost focus before she fell to the floor. Aaron caught her. She came to and grabbed onto him tighter.

He gave a soft smile. "Just a little farther."

She moaned, but kept moving as Aaron guided her.

He helped her stand up before limping into the room. I tensed. It would be hard for them to hurt me in their condition, but doubts inevitably creeped in. What was I supposed to do in this situation?

Heather stood over the bed next to mine. With all those deep gashes, simply being able to stand was impressive.

I watched Aaron pick her up and lay her into bed. He looked at her with calm concern, but also something else. Guilt, maybe.

She winced a couple times and stifled her own screams. My hands bounced anxiously in my lap. She couldn't die after she helped me. Not before I thanked her for giving me my Naomi back, for giving me a piece of my identity that I lost for who-knows-how-long. Not before I got all of the answers I craved.

When Aaron was done, he watched her with an even more dejected expression. "You're such an idiot," he said.

She chuckled. "You're supposed to say, *get some rest, feel bette* —" She clenched her chest in pain.

Aaron almost grabbed her but stopped himself. Eventually, she relaxed on her own.

"Just stop talking, all right? Stay put."

He turned his attention to me. He tried to hide the worry and disappointment on his face, but he didn't do too well.

"What will happen to her?"

He sighed. "We have some healers that can help. One of them is already on his way."

Healers? So, angels could heal after all.

I was taking the angel factor of my memories surprisingly well after stewing in it for a while. What brought about the most anxiety was her. I shivered.

Aaron glanced back at Heather. "And she might heal sooner if her power returns soon."

"Power?" Despite some of my memories resurfacing, I didn't remember anything about the powers angels held, except from what I saw in Aaron's memory.

He turned to me. "Heather has healing powers, too. She could heal herself if..." He glanced away.

I took a guess. "If she didn't use all her power on you?"

He froze before his frown slowly turned into a smirk. "I'm surprised you aren't freaking out right now," he said. "Aren't you scared of all this?"

Actually, I *was* scared. Each time another memory of Naomi invaded my head, my mind became more and more jumbled.

I wasn't sure why I was acting so calm now. Maybe I was just tired, or numb.

"I'm a little surprised myself. My mind feels... It feels so foggy. I can barely focus, except on—"

She and I stood in our field, holding hands. Everyone was watching us, but I didn't feel their gazes. All I noticed was the excitement in her eyes. She was all I wanted to see.

Lady Elisha said something. About soulmates.

We were going to be soulmates. Officially.

I squeezed her hands tighter, but she didn't mind. In fact, she squeezed just as tightly.

Lady Elisha touched our heads and connected us with the link made from a string of light. The soulmate link that would bind us for life.

"It's going to be like that for a while."

Heather. Heather spoke.

For a moment, I was back there with her. But now I was alone. Even with Aaron and Heather in the room, I was completely alone. That shiver creeped in again.

A man rushed inside the room before I could think of an answer. "Is Heather all right?"

The man examined Heather as Aaron said, "She'll be fine with you here."

He must've been a healer then. It was ironic, considering his huge, muscular build.

"I'll start right now." He reached out his dark brown hands. Before I could blink, his palms started to glow with a soft light.

My mouth dropped in awe. The light swirled around her entire body. The wounds slowly closed and her breathing steadied.

This must've been the healing power Aaron was talking about. I didn't know it was so beautiful.

The gigantic man's hands pulled away as the light faded, and Heather sat up on the bed. It was like nothing had ever happened.

She moved her fingers and arms like she was testing them out. "Thanks a lot, Gabriel. I was almost a goner there."

Gabriel chuckled. "I'm just glad you're okay now." He sucked the air in through his teeth. "Now, all you need is some new clothes."

She chortled.

Gabriel turned toward Aaron, but he froze when he caught sight of me. Like he just noticed I was there.

"Caleb?" He walked closer. "Is it really you?"

Caleb? That was what *she* called me.

"*W*HICH ONE DO YOU WANT?"

Naomi had a bunch of books spread out on the table. She'd somehow dragged me into the cramped library. People huddled in groups and read quietly, but it still felt way too crowded.

I scanned the books she picked out for me. "I don't know. I've never really read books before."

"Wow. You're super weird." She picked up a book and handed it to me. "Here."

I ran my finger along the cover. The title read, "The Petals of the Voyager."

"It's a poetry book," she said. "I think you'd like it."

I BLINKED and returned to the room. The man stood in front of me, waiting for my answer.

Caleb. That sounded right. Charles felt like a stranger's name now.

My tense shoulders relaxed, but that shiver didn't disappear. "Yeah, I'm Cale–"

He suffocated me in his grip before I could finish. His hands patted my back. My own arms stayed limp as confusion invaded my body.

He pulled away and placed his hands on my shoulders with a chuckle. "I'm so glad you're alright."

I raised a brow. Even though the answer was clear, I had to ask, "Did I know you?"

"Did I know you?" he repeated with a grin as he pulled his hands off my shoulders. "*Please.* You were the best healer the Sanunduam ever had."

"I was a healer?"

"Of course, you were," he said. "Even when you were little, you were the best healer I'd ever seen."

I was a healer. Adding one more piece to this humongous puzzle made me feel at least a little better.

"I'm so relieved that they got you out of there." His smile softened. Sophistication that he lost mere moments ago sheened in his eyes. "You didn't deserve to be in that place."

Something in his tone touched my heart. If anyone knew where Naomi had gone, it would be him.

"If you knew me, then did you know Naomi, too? Do you know what happened to her?"

What was left of his grin faded. My stomach dropped. "Yes, I knew Naomi. I didn't spend that much time with her, but she was a kind soul."

Was?

"I'm sorry," he said. "I have no idea what happened to her."

I looked away.

That shiver I felt burst into terror. She could've been in danger and... She was using the soulmate connection to call for help. That was what this persistent feeling was. She *was* in danger. Shit.

"Caleb only got a couple of his memories back." Aaron took a couple steps closer. "He still needs time."

Gabriel glanced at him. "Yes, I understand. I'll let you fill him in. I'll make sure the others are okay." His golden eyes peeked at me. "Good to see you, Caleb." Then he walked out and down the long hallway.

So, there were others? How many others?

Aaron pulled out the other chair against the wall and gestured to the chair I'd hopped out of. I reluctantly sat down as he sat down in front of me. He analyzed me with a sympathetic smile.

"So, what else do you want to know?"

I gazed at the floor in thought.

If I was an angel and now I was on earth, that could only mean one thing. "Am I a fallen angel?"

He nodded. "Yes." He pointed at Heather. "Heather and I are fallen angels, too. I fell after, well, you saw what I did."

I was a fallen angel.

"Do you know how I fell?" I asked out of curiosity.

He shook his head. "No. You fell after me, so I have no idea." His lips turned down. "I'm sorry."

Despite that unfulfilling answer, relief followed the disappointment. Before my mind felt shattered. Now that they were giving me answers, it was like I was molding myself back together, albeit a little slowly.

"And how did I lose my memories?"

He scowled. "Anacora stole them."

Anacora. Todd had said that name when he revealed his true colors, and Aaron mentioned him earlier, too. He couldn't be good.

"Who's that?"

"He's a tyrant," he said, disgusted. "He's the Lord, but what He does to angels..." He shook his head. "He believes that redemption is a weak ideal. That second chances shouldn't exist. My faction and I are fighting against that."

"Your faction?"

"We're the Swans," Heather jumped in, already sitting up.

The Swans. That seemed like a fitting name for a faction fighting to become angels again.

"There are two other factions," Aaron continued. "Owls live like mortals among humans. We get along with them most of the time. But the real pain in the asses are the Ravens."

"Aren't those the ones who just attacked you?"

"*Yeah*," he spat with venom in his voice. "They believe that the current God's opinion is all that matters. So, you can see that we don't see *eye-to-eye* right now."

Factions. Factions for fallen angels. Which one was I supposed to be in?

"Any other questions?" he asked.

"Well, um..."

A question instantly came to mind, but I hesitated to ask it. I already knew the answer, but I didn't want it to be true. I desperately wanted to be wrong. I didn't even know why I wanted to be wrong.

"Is—" The word spilled out accidentally, so I kept going. "Is Todd really dead?"

There was silence. A mountain of emotion piled onto me that I thought I'd buried. I hoped and hoped that the answer would surprise me. His silence only added to my anxiety.

He finally said, "I understand why you're upset. I really do. But he was only trying to deceive you to keep you there. Please. Try to understand our reasons."

Todd's body lay on the ground. Blood gushed from his back. He gasped hopelessly for his last breaths. The memory disgusted me.

Honestly, I wasn't sure which part disgusted me the most. Whether I hated Heather and Aaron for killing someone I trusted for so long, or the fact that I was deceived so easily by someone I thought I could trust.

Either way, there was no going back from this. I had to find Naomi. No matter what.

ELEVEN

It had to be night by now. Then again, I didn't really know or bother to find out.

Aaron had rolled out a bed for me. I was too restless to lie in it, though. I wanted to start searching for Naomi right away, but I doubted they had any leads or plans yet. They would've told me otherwise. At least, Gabriel would have.

Aaron had told me he would go outside to watch for any other Ravens. I'd objected, due to his injuries, and the fact that the Ravens were probably targeting him after he killed Todd. He hadn't denied that the Ravens were after him, but he said that he could handle himself. I hadn't stopped him after that. Not after I saw the familiar look of frustrating helplessness and impatience on his face.

I hadn't seen Gabriel either. He was probably busy tending to the wounded. Either that, or he was asleep. I wouldn't bother him or anyone else by stomping around, though, especially because the layout of this place was unfamiliar to me.

"Do you really think other Ravens will come?" I asked Heather, who was as awake as I was.

"I think Aaron only said that to get some fresh air."

I nodded and sunk back into my thoughts. Whenever I spoke to Aaron, he was calm, but he looked so different during the dream. His green eyes were drowned in malice, and his smile was terrifying. He'd killed angels senselessly, all with a grin on his face.

That image seared into my brain terrified me, but it contradicted everything I saw in Aaron. If I hadn't seen him massacring angels with my own eyes, I wouldn't have believed that he'd done it.

"You got his memories, right?" she asked.

I didn't bother confirming. "Why did I get his memories anyway? Why didn't you just give me mine?"

"We couldn't give you your memories there. It was like there was some kind of a forcefield around the town. So, we gave you his instead."

I gazed down at the floor. Remembering Lady Elisha glare at me with those white, glowing eyes gave me goosebumps. I never remembered Her being so terrifying in my own memories.

"Why couldn't you give me yours, or Gabriel's?"

She sucked in air. "Honestly, we thought our memories wouldn't be extreme enough."

"You *what?*"

"With Anacora's influence in you, we had to give you an extreme memory to jumpstart you. Aaron had the most extreme by far."

So, they had shown Aaron's murderous rampage to punch through the fog? Well, it definitely did that...

My eyes dragged to the floor. Knowing that they gave me Aaron's memories for such a purpose gave me mixed feelings. I was both grateful and spiteful that they did, but mostly grateful. I'd put up more of a fuss if I wasn't.

Heather's gaze scrutinized me as I sank deeper in thought.

Aaron. I had to know more about him. Who, or what, could make Lady Elisha so scary?

My eyes darted to her face. "Can you..." But was it okay to ask about his past? Did I even want to know? "...tell me more about him?"

Her eyes wandered to the ceiling. "I know about as much as you. He stole a sword blessed by one of the First Ones, the Galactica, and killed angels with its power. But soon after, he was brought down by Lady Elisha before She died and the sword was taken back."

It clicked. Why the sword felt so powerful in his hands. Why he valued it so much and why it made him mad with power so quickly. But how did it start? Why steal the Galactica in the first place?

"Do you know why he stole it?"

"No." She paused. "It's still hard to believe he did it at all."

"Are you sure he's trustworthy?"

"Definitely not," she said. My eyes rounded. That wasn't the answer I expected. "I mean, you're never *really* sure who you can trust."

I stared at her, mulling over her words. Why did she have to be so cryptic?

She caught my confused expression and explained herself. "I've seen his personality change in a second. I think something bad happened to him that caused it."

"Do you not know what happened? Aren't you guys soul-mates?" That much was obvious by now.

She stiffened. "No, we aren't *really* soulmates. We're not even a couple really, but we've known each other for a long time."

"You guys *aren't* together?"

"No. We're just friends. Really good friends who have known each other for a really long time."

My lips thinned. That denial was not convincing at all. What can of worms did I just open?

I tried steering the conversation back in the right direction. "So, he has two personalities?"

She cleared her throat. "Yes. The main one is calm, caring, and compassionate. The other one is basically pure arrogance and anger. He can be really scary sometimes... but he's never hurt me or any of the others. In fact, he's saved my life so many times, even when he's changed."

I sighed. That explanation led me nowhere.

"I'm sorry if I'm ruining your sleep." I remembered how I'd snapped at her while tied up to the bed. "And I'm sorry for yelling at you earlier."

She laughed–she actually laughed. "It's okay. I wasn't going to sleep anyway. And it wasn't you back there. It was Anacora."

Really? That was why it felt like I was being controlled. That answer didn't settle me, though.

"He can do that?"

"Not anymore. I think he added that as a defense mechanism to stop anyone from giving your memories back." She gave me a reassuring smile. "You don't need to worry."

I pushed out a breath of relief. Then I remembered something, a question I forgot to ask. "Hey, Heather?"

"Yes?"

"Why did Anacora take my memories away?"

Silence swept the room before Heather scooted in her bed. "We have no idea. We think it had something to do with why you fell, but we don't know why you did. The only reason we rescued you was because Gabriel asked us to."

Was that *really* the only reason Anacora took them away? Maybe I did something so terrible that He wanted to punish me more than just making me fall. But wouldn't becoming a fallen angel be enough punishment as is?

"Not that we're not happy we did it," she said. "I know we just met, but you seem like a nice guy."

She thought I was a nice guy? Even if my mind was being messed with, I lit a casino on fire and almost hurt a lot of people. There was no way I could call myself a nice guy. In fact, I couldn't call myself anything. Not until I knew everything about myself.

CHAPTER
TWELVE

"Caleb? Caleb, wake up."

My arm flailed in someone's grip. Every time I drifted back to sleep, they shook my arm harder. I groaned and slowly opened my crusted eyes.

The familiar, dank room greeted me. Heather looked at me with a smile. The green dress she wore was simple, but pretty.

So, I had fallen asleep after all. For a while, I thought I would stay up all night thinking about her and all the holes in my memory.

Heather waited for me to sit up before she glanced across my body. "You should change."

I waited for a laugh, but nothing came out of her mouth. But she had to be kidding. "Uh, I didn't bring along any clothes. You, just..."

"Oh right." She chuckled to herself. "We kidnapped you."

It astonished me. She said that like it was a joke. But it didn't matter. These people were my only chance in finding Naomi. Well, these *angels*.

"Why do I need to change? Where are you taking me?"

After seeing my solemn expression, her smile crumbled. "I was going to take you to meet some more Swans." Her lips curved up in an attempt at politeness, nothing like her natural, joking grin. "But if you don't feel comfortable right now, I won't force you."

Meeting more Swans. Imagining a room full with an army of fallen angels staring at me did indeed make me uncomfortable. An army would definitely help me find her, though.

"Why?" I asked. "Why go through all this trouble for me? I don't even have all of my memories back." That pity-party of a question tumbled out before I could stop it.

"It's because we have to take care of each other." She nodded. "Fallen angels stick together."

I bundled the sheets in one of my palms. "If you say so."

I didn't deserve this kindness. Not after the way I'd treated them after they saved me. Even if it was from Anacora's influence, I was still the one that said those things.

"So?" She analyzed me with questioning eyes. "Do you want to meet them?"

I exhaled in defeat. "Might as well."

"All right," she chirped. "Gabriel and Aaron will be there, too, so don't be nervous." That barely calmed my nerves.

WE WALKED ALONG A LONG HALLWAY. Rooms and doors lined the edges. I peeked into the rooms with open doors. Some of them were filled with food and supplies. One of them was filled with showers. That room made me realize how smelly I was. At least I had clean clothes on now that Heather had given me.

"So," I started, "What are the others like?"

"Well, you already met Gabriel. He's the happy one in the group. Then there's Theo and Ethan—they're twin brothers—and Nathan. Nathan's really shy, and Theo's a nincompoop. Ethan's a clever one, though, which is weird considering Theo's his brother."

I raised my brow. "That's it?"

"Yes. Why?"

"I thought there'd be more. Closer to an army."

She glanced away. "There used to be, but the Ravens have captured or killed a bunch of us. The Swans who weren't caught are scattered across the world."

My heart cringed. Being separated from Naomi was enough to send goosebumps across my skin. I could've only imagined what the pain of losing hundreds, maybe thousands, of comrades in battle was like. "I'm really sorry."

"It's okay," she said. "We've been trying to find out where more Raven bases are so that we can rescue the ones that have been captured. Aaron says that we're close."

"That's good." It was strange that the Ravens wouldn't kill all the Swans they came across, considering how ruthless they seemed to be, but it would've been insensitive to tell her that.

She stopped walking. We'd reached a dead end in the hall. She stared at the steel wall in front of us. "We're here."

Really? The entrance to the room was a wall?

She turned to me. "Remember, just because you aren't initiated, doesn't mean that you aren't welcome. And you can leave anytime. We're rescuers, not kidnappers."

I nodded. So, she was joking earlier after all.

When she turned back to the wall, she widened her legs and placed one hand on the steel. "Pudicitiam."

I stared at the wall in anticipation, but nothing happened. She stood there a while longer, but still nothing. Wasn't something supposed to happen?

My ears caught a ring in the distance, but it wasn't an unpleasant screech. It reminded me of a singing choir. The edges of the wall glowed, like when Gabriel had healed Heather. The light grew brighter and brighter.

I shielded my eyes with one arm. No matter how hard I tried opening my eyes, the light jammed them shut. Then the light was gone.

Heather dropped her hand and the wall split in two. The divided wall slid open, revealing a huge room.

My mouth dropped.

Heather placed her hand on her hip with a grin. "Welcome to the Swan base."

She walked in and I followed. We barely stepped through when I heard the huge wall-door close behind us.

I gazed up at the ceiling that had to be at least three stories high. Instead of being a square, the room was in the shape of a hexagon. Almost every wall was covered in shelves stocked full of weapons—guns, bows, and even swords.

The wall in front of us was the only one without weapons. It sported a gigantic flag that framed the wall. The background was sky-blue. A swan spread its wings out and opened its mouth, ready for a fight.

There were only five other people in the room. Two examined the swords in discussion, one read a newspaper on a table in the middle of the room, Aaron sat next to the boy reading, and Gabriel stood over them. He was the first one who noticed us.

"Hi, Caleb," Gabriel greeted with a grin before waving us over. "Come on over. Don't be shy."

Aaron glanced up as we approached. So did the young man reading the newspaper. His wavy midnight hair was eerily close to Naomi's, but his skin was much lighter and freckles peppered his cheeks. The similar hair must've been a coincidence. My brain found any excuse to think of her. He quickly averted his gaze back to his newspaper.

"How did you sleep, Caleb?" Aaron asked.

"Good enough." I kept falling asleep and waking up, but at least I didn't have any more nightmares.

"Good."

Heather turned to the guys admiring the swords. They hadn't looked at us once. Did they even notice we were here?

"Guys. Stop crushing on the swords and come over here," she said.

They turned around and walked toward us without complaint. They kept talking jibber jabber about steel and other weaponry terms I didn't understand until they arrived at the table.

They had to be the twins Heather had mentioned. They had the same upturned brown eyes, they were the exact same height, and even their buttoned-up shirts were similar. The only difference between them was the shade of their hair. Both had curly locks, but one had hair the color of sand and the other had hair the color of mud.

The only other notable difference was a long scar across the cheeks of the one with lighter hair.

"This is Caleb." Gabriel gestured to me with his palm. "He's the one I mentioned who had his memories taken away."

"Nice to meet you." The twin with muddy hair shook my hand.

"Likewise."

The other brother looked at me strangely. "Didn't Aaron say your name was Charles?"

"It was, but then Heather restored some of my memories, and now it's Caleb."

"Nice," he said with a smirk.

We shook hands as well.

"My brother changed his name to Ethan when we fell, so I understand." That meant he was Theo.

Theo: light hair, long scar. Ethan: dark hair, no scar. I had to remember that.

I looked down at who could only be Nathan. His face went blank. "Uh." His shoulders hunched before he flashed an awkward smile at me. "Hi."

Since he didn't extend his hand for a shake, I did. He stared at my hand for a moment before shaking it. His grip was soft and flimsy, but I didn't mind.

I scanned the group. "It's nice to meet you all. Really."

"And you as well," Theo responded with a smile. The rest nodded.

"So, you don't have all of your memories back?" Ethan asked.

"No."

"Interesting." He methodically placed his fingers on his chin. "The other memories must've been stolen then. Anacora made a huge mistake by not stealing them all. It would only make it easier for people to rescue him." He glanced at Heather. "What was the reason?"

"I have no idea." She seemed troubled by the question. "It was like He wanted us to find him."

I never thought of that. If Anacora wanted to keep me in that strange, fake town in the middle of Kansas, why not steal all my memories? Instead, He blocked a few and stole the rest. Not knowing the answer made me queasy.

Ethan's nostrils wrinkled as his brows sunk deeper. "Anacora isn't the type to take a risk."

"Who cares?" Theo said. "He's one of the most arrogant, self-entitled *Lords* in existence. He probably just wanted to taunt us."

Ethan bounced his head around as he considered the idea. "He *is* becoming more arrogant by the day."

"Exactly. And that's why we have to bring Him down," his brother said.

"We're a long way from that," Gabriel said with a dismissive wave. "We need to focus on finding the Raven bases right now." He glanced at Aaron. "Do you have any info on them?"

"Actually, I do. I got word this morning."

Nathan finally put his newspaper down .

"Spit it out then!" Theo yelled.

Aaron's lips stretched into a grin. "You guys should probably sit down for this."

I glanced at Heather as a reflex. She turned to me with a blank, just-as-lost-as-me expression.

Was the news that huge? Guessing by the half-nervous, half-excited toothless grin on Aaron's face, it had to be.

Everyone quickly sat down, including me.

"All right," he said as if to pump himself up. "I was told where the Tenebris is."

Just when I thought I had some idea of what was happening...

Everyone exchanged rounded glances and surprised gasps, but I did nothing. I had no idea what the Tenebris was. It had to be a Raven base. That much was obvious. But why was it called that? What did that name even mean?

"Where is it?" Gabriel asked.

"Just a little north of a town in Montana. It's around fifteen hours away by car."

Theo shot onto his feet. "Then let's go."

"We need a plan, dumbass," Ethan said while side-eyeing him.

Theo glared at him before begrudgingly sitting back down with his arms crossed. Now I knew what Heather meant when she said Theo was a nincompoop. There was something charismatic about his enthusiasm, though.

"So, what *is* the plan?" Heather asked.

"I was thinking that we could get caught on purpose and break out with the other prisoners," Aaron said with a devilish smirk.

Seriously? That was the riskiest plan I had ever heard. What if the Ravens killed us instead? What if we couldn't break out of whatever this place was?

Aaron continued, "The person's that's been informing me is a telepath, so—"

"Really?" I asked. "Angels can read minds?" I didn't remember being able to do that. Then again, I didn't remember much at all.

"No, but one can communicate through thoughts," Gabriel said. He seemed as stunned as I was. So did the others. "Gods are able to bless inanimate objects, but there was one who tried to bless angels. And telepathy was given to one of those angels."

That alone showed how much of my memory I still hadn't recovered. Such an angel must've been famous.

"Where did you find a mummy like that?" Theo asked.

"Actually, we met before I joined the Swans," Aaron said, barely answering Theo's question. "Anyway, once we break out with the prisoners, we can lead them to the Owl tunnels. From there, they should be safe."

"What are the Owl tunnels?" I asked. "And what the hell is the Tenebris?" It sounded like it was a prison of sorts, but I wanted to know for sure.

"The Owl tunnels are underground tunnels spread across the world that the Owl faction built," Ethan said. "They let fallen angels in from any faction as long as they don't get violent, so most Ravens are banned. And the Tenebris is a Raven stronghold that..." He paused for a moment. "That houses prisoners."

"More like tortures them," Theo muttered.

Torture. The world that I stepped into looked even more dangerous than before.

"Then why don't we use the Owl tunnels to get there?" I asked.

Ethan cringed. His eyes glanced at Aaron before he looked away. My eyes snagged on Aaron for an answer.

"Being out in the open will make it easier to draw the Ravens out. Trust me," Aaron said.

I leaned back. That answer wasn't nearly as satisfying as I

thought it would be, but my brain was too bombarded to ask too many questions.

Theo waved his hand. "You have your plan. Can we go now?" he asked Ethan.

"Not before we eat. You should know better than anyone what happens if you don't eat before a big fight."

"Shut up," Theo pouted. I thought with such a gnarly scar that Theo would be the mature one. But obviously, he wasn't.

"So, what should *I* do?" I asked. There was no way I could fight, and I didn't remember how to heal.

"Come with us if you want," Gabriel said. "I can reteach you how to heal."

They would let me come so easily? I thought they'd keep me here, considering what a huge liability I would be. And there wasn't any reason for me to go anyway. Maybe it would be better if I stayed.

"Can I ask you something?" I said.

Gabriel nodded.

"Since the Ravens are siding with Anacora, are they working with Cloud agents?"

The room turned ghostly quiet. My heartbeat quickened. Their silence told me everything.

"We believe that they are," Aaron jumped in.

Todd was a Cloud agent. He was from the organization founded by Anacora, the same one that kept me in that *place*.

"Would they..." I bit my lip. "Would the Ravens have my memories?"

Gabriel stared deep into my eyes. "Maybe." The conviction in his voice was strong, despite that flimsy word. But even if there was a minuscule chance that they were there, a chance that I could find a clue to find Naomi and save her from whatever she was so afraid of, then I would take it.

"I'm going."

The steadiness in my voice surprised me just as much as it did the others.

Theo was the only one grinning. "That's the spirit," he said. "If you're a healer, I can give you something." His head jerked to the wall behind him, stacked with guns–the same weapon that killed Todd. The memory of his death stirred up feelings of betrayal and loss.

"I thought it would take more than a gun to kill an angel," I mentioned, trying to stop those feelings from growing. "Are the fallen weaker?"

"Uh, no. They're all blessed," Theo said matter-of-factly.

I stared at Theo blankly. I remembered Todd saying that about his sword and Gabriel explaining that Gods blessed inanimate objects, but I had no idea what it really meant. "What does that mean?"

"What?" he shouted. "You're telling me you remember that guns don't do a lot of damage, but you don't know what blessed means?"

I sucked my lips in. Everyone stared at me, and I had no idea what to say. I'd only guessed that a gun wouldn't do much from the fact that angels were supernatural beings, but one had easily killed Todd. I didn't know what to think anymore.

"Blessed weapons are the only things that can fatally harm an angel, fallen or not," Gabriel explained.

"Really?" I took a moment to look around the room at the walls stacked with weapons. Along with amazement came nausea.

"Normally, fighters like us don't even need weapons because of our powers," Ethan said. "But they're useful to have for healers that can't use powers to fight."

"And they're *awesome*," Theo added with a sparkle in his eyes.

"Wait, healers can't use powers to fight?" I repeated.

"No," Heather answered. "And fighters can't use powers to heal, either."

I looked away. While I was frustrated that I couldn't fight using my powers, I was relieved, too. Fighting never came naturally to me, and that fact made sense now that I knew I was a healer. But I would still have to take a gun to this prison break for protection. The thought alone made me sick.

"Well, unless you're Gabriel or Nathan," Theo added with a shrug.

One of my eyebrows shot up. "What does that mean?"

"Nathan and I are balanced, so we can fight *and* heal," Gabriel explained.

"Wow," I muttered. Gabriel was already intimidating with his huge, muscular build. It made sense that he fought, too. I couldn't imagine the spazzy Nathan fighting, though.

"All right," I said, shifting my attention back to Theo. "Thanks for lending me one."

"Happy to help," he said with a nod.

There was so much to take in all at once. Just the amount of information I had to absorb was enough to make me dizzy. But Naomi's fear was much heavier. In a weird way, her fear kept my mind moving. And Gabriel's patient smile kept me sane. Well, somewhat sane.

"I'm guessing we're heading out today?" Heather asked Aaron.

"Yes," he said.

"Then we should start training you to heal right away." Gabriel nodded at me, and I nodded back.

"Finally!" Theo shot up his arms.

Ethan leered at him, and Theo sighed in response. "After breakfast," he pouted.

CHAPTER

THIRTEEN

Gabriel led me through the hallway that I followed Heather through earlier, past the showers and the room I spent the night worrying in, all the way down to the end. At the end of the hall, bars on the wall led up to the top. When we got closer, I noticed the trapdoor on the ceiling. We'd been underground this whole time?

Gabriel grabbed one of the handles.

"Wait." His head turned over his shoulder at me. "We're going outside to train?" I asked.

"Yes."

"But what if there were still Ravens up there? We only got attacked yesterday."

"Don't worry. When Aaron went up yesterday, he scouted the area and saw no sign of Ravens." His golden-brown eyes showed no hesitation, and his warm smile screamed confidence. It spread toward me like a contagious disease.

"Okay."

He swung onto the bars and climbed up to the trapdoor.

When he reached the ceiling, he easily pushed the door open and stepped outside.

"Don't be shy," Gabriel told me from above.

That familiar shiver of Naomi's terror stung me as I touched a cold, metal bar. I had to hurry. I climbed up, just as Gabriel did, and swung my feet onto the ground above.

Pine trees stacked around us. The lush grass was a nice change compared to the dry dirt in that town, or whatever it was. Calling it a prison felt more appropriate now.

Gabriel closed the door, which was camouflaged with grass. As soon as he did, the door turned invisible in the lush. Hopefully he would still remember where it was when we finished.

Gabriel analyzed me with a tooth-filled grin. "Let's begin," he said before rubbing his hands together and speeding away. I followed him, not knowing what else to do. We didn't go far before stopping.

He crouched and looked over his shoulder at me. "Come on down."

I bent down next to him and saw a wilting flower. It looked like it was already dead. Staring at that flower somehow made me think of her, my Naomi. Her own fear prickling at my skin confirmed that she was still alive, but...

"You really don't know what happened to her?" I asked Gabriel one more time.

His eyes softened. "No. I'm sorry."

"Do you know what happened to *me*, though?" The question popped out before I could stop myself. "I mean, do you know how I fell? There's just something that's been bothering me."

The sadness I had tapped in him grew in his eyes. "I think I have an idea, yes. But it's not definite." Before I could ask for more details, his eyes sharpened. "What's been bothering you?"

"It's just..." I glanced away. "I don't understand why Anacora went through all this trouble. Wouldn't being cast out of Heaven be enough punishment by itself?" I rubbed my elbow in pitiful comfort. "Some days, in that place, I felt like I was splitting in two. And like I was repeating the same days over and over. What did I do to deserve that?"

His expression shuttered as he gazed at me—not that he looked indifferent. In fact, he seemed deep in thought. The emotions he felt were a complete mystery to me though.

"I'll tell you after you try healing this little guy." His lips rose. "Promise."

The brown, crusty flower decayed below me.

He was right. I had to learn how to heal again. For Naomi's sake, my questions could wait.

"I'll guide you through it," he said. "Put your hands out towards it." I obeyed him. "And it might be easier if you close your eyes, but it doesn't matter. Whatever you're more comfortable with."

I closed my eyes and breathed in.

"Focus on what you feel around you. Is it hot, cold, humid, dry?"

It was definitely hot. The summer sun kissed my back with refreshing warmth. The crisp air contradicted the moist, humid air of that place. *That place. My prison.* I shivered.

"Now, feel the air around you. Feel the energy."

How was I supposed to do that? And what did that even mean?

A breeze circled around me. That was the closest thing I felt with *"the air around me."* Then again, there was something else, too. Something warm and light. Was it the energy?

"Try to focus the energy into your palm," Gabriel commanded.

I breathed out. The warm sensation traveled to my arms and concentrated into my hands. My palms stung for a moment, but only for a moment.

"And pour it into the flower."

My fingers tensed as I tried shooting the warmth into the flower. A string of energy gently flowed into the wilted bloom. Relief rushed through me before the force snapped back into my hands.

"Fuck!" I flung backwards, opening my eyes and rubbing the middle of my palms. A burning sensation seared them.

"What happened?" Gabriel scooted next to me. "Are you all right?"

The pain faded away. "I don't know." I glanced at the flower. It hadn't changed at all. "It felt like I got shocked. With lightning."

For the first time since I'd met him, Gabriel wasn't smiling. His eyes narrowed in deep concentration. "It backfired," he explained. "Sometimes that happens when fighters try to heal, but that's impossible."

So, I failed? Why? There was nothing stopping me from healing now, so why didn't it work? Maybe I wasn't good enough in the first place. Maybe my powers had faded somehow. Whatever the reason, I failed.

I inhaled deeply. It was a useless attempt at calming myself. All it did was show Gabriel how frustrated and desperate I was. "What should I do now?"

Gabriel analyzed my pathetic demeanor. His eyebrows rose cheekily along with the edges of his lips. "Try again."

"What?"

He grabbed my hand and help me back up. "Try again. Just one more time."

"But—"

"You want to find Naomi, right?" He stared at me expectedly. With hunched shoulders, I slowly, barely nodded. "One more time, then," he said.

Maybe, just maybe, one more try couldn't hurt. I couldn't give up so easily. Not with her counting on me.

He let go and I walked back to the flower, crouched down, put my hands over it, and closed my eyes. I took in a breath before spinning the energy around me.

I guided the light through my arms and into my hands. Then it cascaded into the flower. I grinned with elation before it backfired.

I winced and cursed under my breath. It still didn't work.

"Hmm." Gabriel rubbed his cheek in thought. "I wonder if it's because you don't have any memories of when you healed," he thought out loud. "Maybe it blocked your ability to heal somehow."

That made sense. Still, that meant I had to rely on a gun even more. The thought alone almost made me gag, but that didn't matter. I could've only imagined what Naomi was going through that made her so terrified.

"All the more reason to help everyone." I tried putting on a confident façade, but the tenseness inside me escaped in my voice. "If I need my memories, I have to go, no matter what everyone says."

He looked at me with shocked eyes. But he eventually broke the deafening silence by bursting into laughter. "Who said you weren't going?" he said, still chortling a little.

I gnawed the inside of my cheek. "Well, uh... Wouldn't I be a liability?"

He giggled. "So is Theo, but we bring him along for some reason."

I squinted. What was going on in his head? Gabriel's eyes alone showed his wisdom, the sharpness of his mind, his seemingly endless experience. But that smile and that laugh pushed all that seriousness away.

"Hey." Gabriel shot up his brows with a grin. "If anyone tells you, you can't go with us to find your *own memories*, then they're assholes."

I raised a brow. "Isn't swearing against the bible?"

He let out a quick laugh before patting my shoulder. "If so, then we're both goners."

I frowned after remembering what I said moments ago when the energy backfired. Whoops.

"If only you could see your face right now," he said.

I glanced away with a twinge of embarrassment. Maybe swearing was how I fell. My eyes darted back to him. "You said you'd tell me after. Why I fell."

His cheery smile slowly faded into a thoughtful gaze. I swallowed my fear before he started his explanation.

"This is only a theory," he said. "I fell before you, so keep that in mind."

I nodded.

"I'm sure you don't remember this, but Gods can sometimes get... special abilities. One could control the elements. One could communicate telepathically, until He gave that ability to an angel." That must've been the angel Aaron was getting information from. "And Anacora has one of those abilities."

"Really?"

He nodded. "He's able to control people's minds."

My eyes almost popped from their sockets. He could control minds, and they wanted to beat Him? How could you beat someone who could control your mind?

"And I eventually found out that He was using his ability to do horrible things. And as the founder of the Sanundaum, I knew I had to do something. But He knew I was planning to overthrow Him, so He cast me out before I could. But, I did get the chance to tell *you* before I fell."

"Me?" I pointed to myself. "But why me?"

He smirked. "It's like I said before. You were the best healer we had."

Right, he had said that. And to think, I couldn't even heal a flower now.

"He must've found out I told you, and that's why you fell."

I scrunched my brows. "But why wouldn't He just mind control us to keep our mouths shut? It would've been a lot less work than putting me in some messed up flick town and making you fall."

Gabriel shook his head. "I'm not sure."

I took a minute to soak in what he told me. I thought I did something terrible, but all I did was discover the truth. Strangely enough, it was relieving to know.

"What exactly was He doing?" I asked.

His brows lowered. "You don't want to know. Trust me."

I glanced away for a moment before nodding. Gabriel gave me one of the answers I'd been craving, and that was enough. For now, anyway.

"Thank you."

He stared at me softly before pushing his knuckles into my arm. "Don't thank me yet. We still have to find Naomi."

A tiny smile popped onto my lips. At least I wasn't alone in my search.

FOURTEEN

"You can't heal?"

Everyone sat at the table in the underground bunker they called their base, eating the breakfast Ethan had mentioned before. Gabriel and I had sat down and told them what had happened. Heather spoke out first.

"No," I said. "I'm sorry."

All that answered my apology was silence until Theo opened his mouth.

"Psh." He waved his hand. "Who needs healing when we have guns?"

Guns. I was going to have to shoot someone, wasn't I? Nothing filled me with more dread. Well, *almost* nothing. That cold warning was still there, at the edge of my mind, crawling on my skin. I had to find her. Fast.

Ethan sighed. "He *is* right, though. With a weapon, you should be fine."

I blinked. "Really?"

"We'd be assholes if we didn't let you come," Aaron said with a smirk.

"Yeah." Heather looked away in thought. "It surprised me, is all."

"I..." Everyone turned to Nathan, who spoke his first word since I'd met him. Heather *did* say he was shy. "I think you're right, though, Gabriel." He turned to Gabriel, who sat in between Nathan and I, but he didn't quite look him in the eye. "So, if we find his memories there, then he should be able to heal?"

"Yes," Gabriel responded.

Nathan's lips quirked as he looked away. "Good."

Theo jumped onto his feet and hopped toward me like a kid during Christmas. "Come on. I'll give you one of my babies."

He dragged me up from my seat and to the shelves stacked with guns.

I PACKED some clothes they gave me into a random backpack they had. They said the trip would take two days by car so that everyone, including the driver, was well-rested when we arrived, but that felt like forever with Naomi's life on the line.

I had tried to ignore that nagging foreboding to concentrate on all the information that had been piled onto me, but it wasn't easy. Naomi's fear was intense at times, bursting through my own emotions. I had no idea what she was so afraid of, but her call was enough to tell me that she wasn't safe. That she needed me. *She needs me.*

"Caleb?"

I flinched. The room I spent the night in materialized around me as well as the shirt in my hands.

I turned to the hallway where the voice came from. Nathan stood there, holding his hands awkwardly in front of him. That was exactly what Naomi did when she was nervous.

"Yes?" I asked.

"I..." He paused. "Well, I..." His eyes darted to the side. "Can I talk to you?"

My brows scrunched together. Wasn't that what he was doing? "Yes. Of course."

He almost took a step into the room before stopping himself. His lips squished to the side awkwardly before he committed to entering the room.

He forced a smile before it quickly vanished. "Hi."

"Hi?"

What did this spaz want? It seemed like whatever Nathan wanted to tell me had to be important. Why else would he have such a bad case of the zorros?

"Okay." He shook his head. "My sister... she knew you before."

"Before I fell?"

He nodded.

I placed the shirt back onto the bed, my own curiosity leading me to ask, "Did she tell you what I was like?"

He smiled again, this time softer. "Yeah. She said... she said you were the best thing that ever happened to her."

His words froze the air in my lungs. It couldn't be. Was his likeness to her not a coincidence after all?

I stomped toward him. "What was your sister's name?"

He locked eyes with me. His irises were umber, close to black, drastically contrasting her sandy brown eyes. Still, something about them was all too recognizable.

"Naomi," he said.

I stepped back. Something snapped. My heart smashed against my ribcage. Adrenaline pounded through my entire body as my breaths narrowed. Faster. Faster.

"Caleb?"

I crashed onto the ground, leaning against the bed. Thousands of fire ants bit into my skin. Every part of me was trembling. I heaved in shallow breaths.

"Caleb!" Nathan's face appeared in front of me. His mouth moved, and he said my name, but it wasn't in his voice. Naomi?

"Caleb." His mouth didn't move at all that time. It was her voice, calling out to me. "Caleb!"

Naomi. This was Naomi's fear, spreading to me.

My arms wobbled against my chest. My sharp breaths were the only things louder than my pounding heartbeat. Her call had never been this intense.

"Caleb." Nathan snatched my hands. "Try to relax your shoulders."

My shoulders squeezed against my neck. I slowly forced them back down, heaving like a maniac.

"Now breathe in through your nose, out through your mouth."

My arms trembled furiously in his grip as I did what I was told. In through my nose: out through my mouth. In: out. In, and out.

After a couple more long minutes of steadying my breathing, my body relaxed. Still, my mind couldn't completely settle now. Whatever was happening to her, it was getting worse. Much worse.

"Are you all right?" Nathan studied me with growing concern.

I took one more second to compose myself and nodded. "Yeah. Yeah, I'm fine."

He released me as I stood up and sat onto the bed. Nathan stood up as well, keeping a close eye on me. "Are you sure?"

I bit my lip and nodded again.

He narrowed his eyes. "What happened?"

I glanced at the floor, hesitating to reveal what just happened. How I'd just acted in front of a practical stranger was so embarrassing. But she was his sister. He deserved to know. I had to swallow my pride and tell him.

"Naomi." Nathan carefully sat down next to me with the backpack between us. "She's been calling out to me."

"Really?" he asked, excitement in his voice. "Do you know where she is?"

I squinted. "So, you don't know either, huh?"

His grin dropped into a frown. "I guess not."

I groaned from a mix of anger and helplessness and looked to the ceiling, propping my arms behind me for support. "All I feel from her is fear. If only I knew where she was, then I could save her. But..." I cringed, not having the heart to finish the sentence.

"That's why we're going to the Tenebris." He looked at me with a new confidence in his expression. "That's why you're coming, right? You're hoping to find some of your memories? I think there's a good chance they're there. What better place to hide them than in a super-secret stronghold?"

One side of my mouth rose into a goofy half-smile. "You think so?"

He nodded.

WE DROVE ON THE ROAD. An actual paved one. I was so used to dirt roads that I expected a bump every other second and was shocked when it didn't happen.

There was a pistol in my lap. An actual gun. I hadn't really listened to Theo's lecture on guns. All I focused on was how to reload and shoot, which was all I needed to know.

It sickened me. Just having a gun close to me made my stomach whirl and I had no idea why.

"So, how long have you been down here?" Nathan asked.

I looked up.

Everyone had been separated into two cars. I was put with Aaron, Theo, and Nathan. I was indifferent to the arrangements, except with Nathan. Ever since he opened up about his sister, he didn't act nearly as awkward around me.

"I have no idea," I answered.

Nathan's brows curled with guilt. "I'm sorry."

"It's okay. I don't remember a lot anyway."

"Yeah, Nathan." Theo was in the passenger seat up front. His body turned toward us. "It's not your fault that Anacora's an asshole."

Nathan's eyes rounded for a moment before blush splashed his face. He glanced down and ignored Theo completely.

Theo's eyes narrowed before he smirked at me. "So, you've been down here and didn't know anything about guns? I think you're the first man in the twentieth century who doesn't."

I chuckled. "I suppose. It just didn't feel right." Maybe that was why I felt sick from having one in my lap.

"My sister said you were nice," Nathan said. "Said you wouldn't hurt a fly."

"Naomi said that?"

"Yeah. And—" His voice cracked as a glaze overtook his eyes.

"And what?" I prodded, desperate for any information about Naomi.

He shut his eyes. "Never mind."

I wanted so badly to know more about her, but by the expression on her brother's face, it wasn't a happy memory. I wouldn't make him uncomfortable by pressing.

"Just spit it out, Nathan," Theo commanded.

"I don't want to talk about it."

"But—"

"Theo!" Aaron spoke up. "If Nathan doesn't want to talk about something, you should respect his wishes."

Theo shrank in his chair and turned back around, sulking like a ten-year-old. "Yeah, okay, sorry Nathan."

Nathan hunched over.

Ignoring the childish strain, I looked at the gun, feeling sicker than ever. We'd only been driving for a couple hours, and I was already terrified. Not just of dying, but of killing another person. Would I be able to pull the trigger? Would I be of any use at all? Was this a mistake?

But this wasn't just for my memories—this was for her. I had to bear it.

~

Sleeping in cars never bothered me. I'd done it a couple times before. But this time, I couldn't fall asleep. Even though the blanket I had was really soft and my eyes felt like they were falling off my head, sleep eluded me.

The Ravens at the Tenebris were supposed to be the worst of them all, and we were going to be captured *willingly*. I'd tried to keep my nerves at bay, but that was impossible.

I was going to a fight without knowing how to fight, without *wanting* to fight. And yet, all it took was her sandy brown eyes to convince me there was no other choice. This was my only lead.

We were in Montana now. It was much more beautiful than Kansas. Then again, I couldn't see much of it in the darkness.

We pulled into a parking lot in some random town. I'd almost forgotten what a parking lot even looked like.

"*Pst...*" someone whispered. "Caleb? Are you awake?"

I rolled over and saw Theo staring at me from the passenger seat.

"Theo?" I mumbled. "What is it?"

"Does..." He grabbed his arm and rubbed it nervously. "Does Nathan hate me?"

"Why would you think that? And how should *I* know?" Despite our quick connection, Nathan and I had only just met.

"I'm sorry. I know it's a weird question. It's just..." A forlorn expression settled over his face, and I sat up. This was going to take a while. "He's been here for a while now, and he's at least warmed up a *little* to everyone. Everyone but me." He leaned closer. "And *you*. You made him talk to you even though you just met. How did you do that?"

"I didn't do anything. He just talked to me."

"Oh." He gazed at the dashboard. "So, he *doesn't* like me."

"But why would he—"

"Everyone tells me I'm too reckless. My own brother tells me *constantly*. He tells me to shut up and listen for once, but I never can." His gaze shifted to Nathan, who was sound asleep. "And Nathan is the exact opposite of me. It's pretty obvious why he hates me."

I furrowed my brows, trying to come up with a response that would please him. "Just because he doesn't talk a lot, doesn't mean he hates you."

When he didn't answer, I asked, "Have *you* ever tried starting a conversation?"

"Well, yeah," he said, his tone indignant. "I've tried talking to him multiple times. You saw what happened today."

I shook my head. "But did you tell him something about yourself?"

He scratched his chin. "I mean, no. Not really."

"Why not?"

His lips flattened into a grimace. "'Cause it could get awkward."

"Exactly. I bet Nathan feels the same way. So, if you want him to talk to you, maybe try telling him something about yourself," I lectured. Why was he asking *me* of all people about this anyway?

He stared at me blankly then scowled. He spun around so that he faced his window and threw the blanket over him.

"Yeah, okay," he said sarcastically. "Thanks for nothing."

What was his problem?

I sighed as the shiver crawled down my back, making the end of my breath shaky. Maybe I would never fall asleep.

WE WERE OFFICIALLY OFF-ROADING. All I had in my stomach was the beef jerky and bacon we brought with us.

Pine and oak trees gazed down on us from above. Mountains towered in the distance. If the circumstances were different, this place would've been great for camping, but that was a silly thought now.

Despite my calm appearance, internally I was freaking out. Even if Naomi was beyond worth doing this for, I still had no clue what I was doing.

We stopped. Aaron got out of the car, followed by Theo. Nathan and I trudged along behind them after exchanging a glance.

"Are we there?" I asked.

"Not quite. We're about five miles away, but even that's risky. We have to meet up with the others before we get closer," Aaron answered.

"Sounds like a plan," Theo said with a beaming smile.

It sounded like he was back to his normal, childish self after some sleep. Thank goodness.

"All right. Let's go," I said.

"Yeah," Nathan added. "For the Swans." And his sister.

CHAPTER
FIFTEEN

Dense forest surrounded us. We veered around the shrubs and trees. And the deeper we went, the thicker it became.

The only thing that broke the silence was the occasional tweet or caw from a bird. Maybe they were ravens. That would've been ironic.

"I believe in you," Nathan whispered.

He strolled next to me with a polite smile, and all I could think about was her. This was her little brother. Except for the freckles on his nose, his lighter skin, and his dark brown eyes, their features looked identical.

I gave him a quick smile in return, but I couldn't stop worrying. What if I was too late? That cold dread had disappeared when I woke up this morning and I hadn't felt it since, but I didn't have the heart to tell Nathan. I still held onto the slim chance that she was alive. She had to be.

"I see them," Theo blurted.

The forest thinned out ahead. In between the tree trunks, I saw the rest of the Swans with the other car. Gabriel looked more serious than usual, Heather stared off into space, and Ethan concentrated on something.

"Hi, guys." Theo waved his arms.

Their heads swiveled toward us.

"How are you guys doing?" Aaron asked as we approached.

"We're all right," Heather said.

"Is everyone ready then?" Ethan chimed in.

"Hell, *yeah*," Theo said.

Ethan laughed at his optimism, but I thought he was bonkers.

"So, how is this going to go again?" Heather asked.

"It's simple," Aaron answered. "We walk into their territory, we get ambushed and captured, and we help the other prisoners escape with us."

She nodded, exuding confidence.

I squeezed my eyes shut. Their confidence helped, but the uncertainty inside me didn't go away.

"Yeah," I said, mostly to try and convince myself that it would be okay.

Someone slapped their hand on my shoulder. I opened my eyes and there Heather was. "Just stay close to us. You'll be fine."

This horrible thought of Naomi being gone swarmed through my head, and I wasn't sure if I'd feel better. Not until I knew Naomi was alive. But I nodded, hoping that was enough to convince her that her words assured me.

She removed her hand.

"Let's go," Ethan said.

Everyone nodded and followed Aaron who led the way to the Tenebris.

The gun Theo gave me hung in a holster on my hip. It felt unnatural on me—heavy. Like it was dragging me down.

We walked along a path of sorts for several minutes. It was made of grass and wide enough for all of us to walk side-by-side. It didn't look man-made–or angel-made, I supposed—but it could've easily been made to look natural.

Each step made my spine tremble. I glanced at Nathan. He stared straight ahead with an unreadable expression on his face.

My worrying thoughts swarmed around me. What would I even do if Naomi were dead? Merely being separated from her tormented me. If she were dead, what was the point of all this?

I bumped into something. A hand. Gabriel raised his arm to stop me. I surveyed the team. All of them stood frozen. Aaron searched frantically for something, or someone.

Were the Ravens here? But where?

I searched desperately but I couldn't see anyone. What were they so worried about?

My heart stopped in my chest as a familiar shiver bombarded me. Naomi was alive!

People jumped out of the trees and blocked our path. The Ravens were here after all. They had no weapons, but the malice in their gazes was enough to pierce through me.

"Kill the Swan scum!" one of them yelled.

Theo grinned. "Feisty. I like it."

He swung his arm and a sword of light appeared. He could do that? Theo charged toward them with a battle cry. The sword grew when he raised his arms. He smashed the sword toward the ground and caught two Ravens under the blade. They struggled to block his attack.

The other Ravens sprinted toward Gabriel, but Ethan stopped their advance using a sword like Theo's.

One Raven still snuck through, a sadistic smile on her face.

"Hello, Grandpa," she said to Gabriel.

Light covered her hand as she formed a fist. She cocked her arm. Gabriel didn't move.

She punched. Gabriel caught her fist easily with one hand. She screamed when he flung her into the air.

Damn.

Another Raven caught her when she landed. He lay her down and hovered his hands over her. Light spun in his palms. He was a healer. *Amazing.*

"Gabriel!" someone yelled. The stranger stalked toward him.

My eyes widened. This Raven looked *exactly* like Gabriel. But even though he was smiling, there was something different about it from Gabriel's. Something *menacing.*

"Long time, no see," Gabriel's twin said.

Gabriel squeezed his hand in anticipation.

A white light beamed in the corner of my eye. Aaron blasted a Raven with a laser. The Raven flew back and landed on the ground, unconscious.

The stranger who looked identical to Gabriel widened his eyes and charged toward Aaron. The Raven soared above him before Aaron could react. My heart stopped.

Gabriel punched his look-alike's side, sending him sliding across the grass. But the Raven recovered fast and sprinted to his new opponent. When he got close to Gabriel and threw a punch, they disappeared.

I gasped. They were *that* fast?

Now, Aaron fought alongside Theo, who already had three opponents stacked against him. In such a short time, it had gotten so chaotic.

"Aren't we supposed to do something?" I asked Heather and Nathan. Both focused intensely on the fight.

"Just stay close to me," Heather answered without looking away.

I gawked at her. Despite my fear, I'd agreed to fight, not let them take the punches.

"We're healers," Nathan jumped in after seeing my face. "If *we* get injured, it's over."

"What he said," Heather said.

"But—"

"Focus!"

I had no choice.

Ethan joined forces with his brother while Aaron fought one-on-one with the enemy. A few Ravens lay unconscious on the forest floor. But weren't we supposed to be captured? This seemed like a shit plan.

Aaron fired lasers at a Raven. He dodged them gracefully with a smirk on his face. When he saw an opening, the Raven shot a laser into Aaron's stomach. The impact sent him soaring backwards. Toward us.

Heather caught him and set him on the ground to start healing.

When I looked back at the battlefield, I saw the same Raven preparing to fire the laser at Heather and Aaron. They would aim a laser at healers?

My heart pounded in my chest as I walked toward them and into the line of fire. The memory of Todd's dying breath echoed in my mind. I'd tried to save him just like this. Hopefully, these people were more trustworthy than he was.

The Raven's rage was reflected in his clenched jaw and narrowed eyes. He hated them. He hated *us*.

But his eyes widened in shock after I walked in front of my new friends. The light in his palm fizzed into nothing. He stumbled backwards and turned his attention elsewhere.

Why hadn't he taken the shot? Why did he have such a strange reaction after seeing me? It didn't matter. I saved someone. Finally.

"Caleb," Heather said. "You didn't have to—"

The Raven I scared lay on the forest floor. Someone pinned him down with his foot and leaned close to him.

Gabriel.

His clothes were barely affected by the fight he'd apparently won. It shouldn't have been surprising that he won, but when he disappeared, I worried about him.

I exhaled a huge breath of relief, but it was cut short when I noticed his different clothes.

"Don't you dare kill *any* of them."

That didn't sound like Gabriel. His voice was deeper, if only slightly.

Shit.

He stood and picked the other Raven up by the collar to shove him away.

It was the man Gabriel had been fighting. Gabriel didn't have a beard, but this man did. His hair was so dark that I hadn't noticed it before.

The real Gabriel appeared in front of me with a gust of wind. Slashes oozing blood covered his entire body. The bottom half of his pants and one sleeve were torn, revealing his bleeding skin.

His twin snarled. "How dare you go against God, Gabriel. You were once a supporter. But as soon as Anacora revealed your treachery, you turned. Just. Like." He snapped. "*That.*"

Gabriel heaved. "I believed in the First Ones. I believed in the other Gods as well. But *not* that sinner that calls himself holy."

The Raven glared at him.

I surveyed the battle. Ethan and Theo were on the ground. Blood saturated the grass beneath them. Terror gripped me. No. They couldn't be dead. Aaron said it would be fine. Everyone had.

"Right," Gabriel's twin responded sarcastically. "So, you joined forces with the angel killer and all the *Swan scum.*"

It wasn't hard to figure out who that first nickname was for—Aaron.

I glanced at him, laying in Heather's lap. He breathed slower than usual, but he was still conscious. He gave me a wobbly smile when his eyes found mine.

Nathan glanced at Aaron and me. Frustration strained his face.

"Don't... Nathan..." Aaron warned.

But time froze when Nathan saw the twins bleeding out on the ground. His tense stretched-out palms curled into fists. He sprinted toward them.

Gabriel threw his arm out and stopped him. Nathan gawked at him for a moment before gaining his composure.

To think just tossing out his arm stopped a sprint like that. It was incredible.

Gabriel's evil twin chuckled. "Oh? You aren't even going to let him help your—" The Raven's mouth dropped open as he glanced over his shoulder.

All of us stiffened as we watched the brothers sit up. Both of them. Theo had the same, goofy grin on his face as always, while Ethan was as confused as the rest of us.

Nathan froze. With that much blood loss, they shouldn't have been conscious, even if they were angels.

"Not when I already did," Gabriel said.

The Raven slowly turned his head back to Gabriel. "Your transferring gift is bothersome," he frowned. "But I know it comes at a big price with all your..." He scanned Gabriel from head to toe. "*Injuries.*"

Gabriel collapsed.

"Gabriel!" Nathan screamed. He pounced onto his knees and started healing him, but Gabriel's heavy breathing wasn't improving.

I slowly reached out my hand. I wanted to help, but I was shaking. Literally shaking. What could I do? I couldn't heal.

"Gabri—"

Nathan and Heather crashed into trees. I caught a dark blur following them.

"And Caleb." The Raven appeared in front of me. "I always knew you weren't loyal."

He knew me, but that didn't help. He only looked at me with contempt and anger, and I already hated this guy back. I couldn't forgive anyone that hurt Gabriel.

He scoffed. "You only joined the Sanandum so you could protect that whore!"

I stopped breathing.

"She always followed you like a yapping lap dog. The bitch had nothing else going for her, I suppose."

Naomi. This bastard just called Naomi a whore.

I pulled out the gun and aimed it at his head. Ethan screamed, but his words escaped me. I punched the trigger and the gun recoiled.

He never should've called her that.

I lowered the pistol to my side. The Raven stood there with those same hateful, golden eyes.

In the corner of my vision, Theo's eyes opened wide on his now-pale face. What could get Theo of all people that scared?

I looked down at my stomach. Blood soaked my shirt, but not a single hit struck me. At least, that was what I thought.

The Raven raised his chin. Not a single injury was on him. How? He was right in front of me, in front of the gun.

I fell to the floor.

"Caleb!" A voice. It sounded so far away.

My stomach wrenched with pain. The familiar pain of getting punched mixed with the unfamiliar pain of what I imagined a venomous snake bite felt like. My beating heart added another layer of discomfort. With each pound, more blood spilled out.

I put my hand on my stomach to stop the bleeding, but my

strength was fading. The confusion as to where and when and how I got attacked only piled onto the shock.

"You shoot me, and karma will come for you." He took in a huge breath. "*I have God on my side, Caleb!*"

My ears rang. He must've known his shouting brought me pain, whoever this asshole was.

He walked back to his comrades, turning into a big, dark blur as the world spun around me.

"Tie them up."

CHAPTER

SIXTEEN

Soreness spread through each muscle fiber in my back. I lay down on something hard, like metal or wood.

I opened my eyes and blinked until my foggy vision cleared. Heather crouched over me. Light swirled around her hands and into my wound.

Wait. When did I get injured?

"Careful. He's awake," Aaron said.

Heather pulled her hand away. "All right," she murmured. "That's the best I can do. He can't move around too much or the wound will reopen."

What wound was she talking about?

"You only joined the Sanandum to protect that whore!"

The memory of our capture slowly came back to me. He'd shot me. I didn't know how, or when, but that Raven shot me. The blood stain was on my shirt to prove it. But now, the wound only felt like a sore muscle.

Heather gave me a reassuring smile, but the bags under her eyes contradicted the confidence she fought to portray. Her power was at its limit.

I propped myself on my elbows and slowly edged up the wall behind me. We were trapped in a prison cell insulated with rugged bricks. Straw and dirt covered the ground, insulating the cell with dust. Ethan and Theo sat next to the steel bars keeping us locked inside. Nathan sat against the wall diagonal from me, while Aaron was next to me and Heather.

"Where are we?" I asked.

"We're in the Tenebris," Heather answered. "They blindfolded us before we went inside, so we have no idea what the layout looks like."

Theo eyed the walls. "Except for the layout of this cell."

My hands grazed my holster, but it was empty. Of course, the Ravens would confiscate weapons. I shouldn't have been alleviated with that thing being gone, but nevertheless, I was.

I scanned the cell one more time, but I caught no sign of him. "Where's Gabriel?"

Ethan's eyes narrowed at the floor. "He got *special* treatment."

"What?" A stabbing pain surged through my stomach. I winced. "Why?"

Nathan snapped his eyes toward Ethan. Ethan looked away, but he caved in with a sigh. "Okay. You and Nathan probably don't know this, and it's pretty easy to guess, but... That guy that Gabriel was fighting. That's his brother."

Well, that much was obvious. That guy was an exact replica of Gabriel, except for that smile. Gabriel's grin was warm and inviting. The Raven's smile was malicious, though that single word didn't begin to describe it well enough.

Nathan's face contorted in confusion. "*That's* what you were hiding from me? Why?"

He shrugged. "I wasn't sure if I was supposed to be the one to tell you. No one else spoke up about it."

Theo let out a "hah" sound. "You were overthinking it. As usual."

Ethan scoffed. "Then why didn't *you* tell him, smartass?"

Theo peeked at Nathan. "Um..." He glanced away. "I don't know."

"Bull*shit*," Ethan barked.

To think that Gabriel's brother was a Raven. It was obvious that they had a dark history from the hatred Gabriel's brother harbored toward him. Hopefully, even with all that hatred and animosity inside that Raven, Gabriel was still alive.

"Calm down, guys," Aaron said. "Why are you so angry anyway?"

"Because we got captured and we have no idea where anyone is. I'd probably be a lot calmer if Gabriel wasn't shuffled off to who-knows-where," Ethan screamed.

"Damn," Theo said. "I wish you'd yell more often."

"It's not hard when you're around!"

That interaction put a tiny smile on everyone's faces, but the distraction quickly blipped away.

I shivered, Naomi's fear prickling my skin along with my own, and Heather noticed.

"I healed you to the best of my abilities, Caleb," Heather said. "I'm sorry."

"It's all right." I smiled. She must've thought my shivers came from physical pain. Maybe it would've been better if it was. "It feels a lot better. Thank you."

Judging from her expression, I managed to convince her I was fine, but my emotions were churning into bitterness. The plan that I was questioning from the beginning backfired. Still, I had to hold out in this crazy ride. For Naomi.

"So, we can't bust out of here?" I asked hopefully.

Aaron stood up and bent his legs into a fighting stance. "Watch this." A whip of light extended from his arm.

He slashed at the bars relentlessly, pounding at them over and over. Dust filled up the cell. I squinted until he finished his assault.

When the dust settled, my pupils shrunk. There wasn't a single scratch on them.

"The walls of the cell absorb any energy with malicious intent. That includes when we try to break out."

He lowered his arm and the light disappeared. Even with that blank expression on his face, the shame in his eyes was clear as he sat back down, right next to Heather.

"Aaron?" Heather spoke, exhaustion clinging to her voice. "How are we going to find them? Even if we do find a way out..." Her gaze wandered to the ground.

She was right. Even if we did find a way out, we would still have to search blindly for the prisoners. Then, we would have to escape with an entire crowd of prisoners on our backs. What kind of an insane plan was this?

Everyone looked to Aaron for an answer. After the pressure stacked up in the room, something snapped in his eyes. "How long are you going to sleep?" Aaron yelled to someone. "Or are you just ignoring us?"

Everyone stared at him awkwardly. Silence was the only thing that answered him. Was he messing with us? At a time like this?

"Both," someone answered in annoyance. The voice came from outside our cell. A man's voice.

My head cocked at the sound, but I couldn't see the voice's owner in the dim torchlight.

"Who the hell are *you*?" Theo asked.

"The name's Paul." The voice definitely came from the cell in front of us.

A figure stepped forward. His brown beard was shaggy and untamed. His eyes were understandably jaded with stress. Sleep had to be hard to come by here.

Paul leaned into the bars of his cell. His beige, faded clothes were ragged with holes. His long hair and beard were untamed, proof of his long stay here. "And I'm a spy for Aaron."

He must've been the intel Aaron was talking about. Why didn't Aaron mention him sooner?

I gazed at Aaron. That sinister shadow in his eyes was still there. That dark glint. Did no one else notice it?

"Ha! Not a good one apparently," Theo teased.

"Shut up, ankle biter."

"Hey, I'm not an ankle biter. I've been an adult for over one hundred years, asshole."

Ethan rolled his eyes. "I wish you'd act like one."

Theo crossed his arms in brooding. "Shut up."

"So, this guy is your contact?" Heather asked.

"Yes. He's an undercover prisoner. It was my idea. Amazing, right?" Aaron bragged.

Heather subtly leaned back and away from him. She must've noticed the change in Aaron, too. It wasn't my paranoia then. Also, wouldn't being a prisoner put his intel at a major disadvantage? "Yeah. Good idea, Aaron."

"Of course, it is. So don't freak out. You've got me, so every-thing's going to be fine." Even those words of comfort were satu-rated with arrogance.

"So, you have a plan?" Ethan interjected. "On how to bust us out, I mean."

He glared at Ethan. "You'll know soon enough." His eyes slit. "So just *keep your mouth shut.*"

Ethan pressed his lips into a thin line and said nothing more.

Aaron looked at the spy. "Who's on board, Paul?"

He shrugged. "Around eighty percent of the prisoners I'd say. Which is about eight hundred."

Eight hundred? How big was this place?

"The coup is tonight, by the way," Paul added casually.

"Good. Because we're finishing this mission *successfully.* No matter what." Ice coated Aaron's voice. It was nothing at all like his usual assuring tone.

Footsteps approached us. A woman with shorts and a torn up shirt approached our cell.

"I see you're all enjoying your new home?" she taunted. "You Swan *scum*. Attacking us on our own territory."

Aaron growled with impatience. "*We* aren't the scum here."

Her eyes flashed with anger before she smiled. "You're coming out first." She pointed at him, as if we didn't already know who she was talking about. "You should've kept your mouth shut."

Instead of showing regret, a devilish grin painted Aaron's face.

The Raven frowned. It was difficult to tell if she was angry that her threat didn't work, or confused from his reaction. Perhaps she felt both.

SEVERAL HOURS PASSED and Aaron still wasn't back. I could only imagine what they were doing to him. Lashes? Gouging? Burning?

"I hope he's all right," Heather said. Her dark eyes reflected despair.

I began, "So was that—"

"Yes," she answered me. "It usually happens when we're in danger."

That evil, condescending aura; that piercing stare. It was horrible to admit, but I was relieved once that version of Aaron was taken away. That didn't mean I didn't worry for him, though.

"Are you talking about the change?" Ethan asked.

"Yes," Heather said.

Nathan bent his knees to his chest. "It still freaks me out."

"Same here," Theo said. "There's nothing we can do about it, though."

"Nothing at all?" I pressed.

Theo shook his head with a frown. Even the eccentric actor didn't have any hope.

A pained scream echoed around the prison. Everyone tensed. There had been screams, but it had been quiet for a while, and I hoped it would stay that way for Aaron's sake. But apparently, the Raven wasn't done with him yet.

"Aaron..." Heather choked.

I never thought about any kind of torture, never mind a session this long. Imagining it now made my stomach churn and my blood curl.

"He'll be fine." We looked at Paul, who sat cross-legged inches from the bars of his cell. "If he told me the truth, then you have some great healers amongst you."

The memory of my failure to heal burned in my head. I was the only healer who couldn't heal. Saving Naomi seemed so much harder than before. I desperately wanted my memories so that I could do something—anything.

"Maybe," Heather said. "But he still has to go through this. All for something he has no control over."

"Paul's right, Heather. I know how you feel, but healing is all we can do for him," Nathan comforted.

I lowered my head in shame. *Failure. Worthless.* Those words and a million synonyms bashed my head in. "I wish I could help."

Heather put her hand on my leg. "Don't feel too bad. You aren't the only healer here, you know?"

Her eyes were red from tears and fatigue. Even so, she was trying to cheer me up.

Aaron's scream punched through my ears. His agonized cry soon turned into venomous, taunting laughter. Chills ran up my arm.

"You think a couple of lashes can break *me?*"

The crack of a whip made him scream louder. Each hoarse breath echoed throughout the lair.

"I feel bad for him." Theo played with his thumbs. "Usually, I'm the chatterbox."

"It isn't your fault, Theo," Ethan said. "He made a mistake."

Theo's eyes locked onto the floor. "Yeah. Okay."

Paul grunted. "He says he's fine. Stop worrying."

"You're talking to him right now?" Theo asked, hope returning to his voice.

"Yeah, I *was*. Anything's better than listening to you lot complain."

I analyzed Paul's features closely out of curiosity. His light brown hair flowed down to his shoulders. His tangled beard was untamed and curled in infinite directions. He had been down here for a while, or he hadn't bothered to groom himself.

"Sorry for waking you up earlier," I said out of politeness.

"Don't worry about it." He looked off to the side. "I wasn't going to sleep anyway."

His eyes cringed at the mention of the word sleep. That could've meant only one thing. Nightmares.

"Move!"

That voice. It belonged to the woman who had taken Aaron away.

We saw Aaron first, then the sadistic Raven behind him. She gripped his hands behind his back. He hunched over in pain, but that maddened smile plagued his face. His shirt was gone revealing his back and chest butchered with lacerations. How could anyone stand that much pain?

She opened the creaking cell door and tossed him in by his pants. He didn't move from that spot after, like a corpse. His blood trailed from his back onto the straw-lined floor.

"Aaron!" Heather crawled toward him. She went to touch a cut on his back before stopping herself.

"Your friend there really wanted a good beating." The Raven surveyed us with an evil eye. "Consider yourselves lucky."

I stared at Aaron as his blood gathered below him. He only tried to protect us, and this was his reward.

Other Ravens walked up to our cell and carelessly dropped trays of food for each of us.

"Oh, yeah. Here's your food," she said. "Try not to puke it back out."

They walked away. The bitch's cackle trailed behind her and haunted our cell.

"Aaron? Are you okay?" Heather asked. "Please answer me."

Everyone huddled around him.

He chuckled. "Are you kidding? *She* was the one that couldn't break me."

His tone didn't sound like he was bluffing or being sarcastic at all. His alter ego was still in charge after everything that had happened.

Heather raised her hand above his back. Instead of healing, she followed through with what she almost did earlier and grazed one of the wounds. Aaron winced. She immediately pulled away with an apology.

With his flinch, his smirk turned into a gritting frown. The shadow, or whatever it was, retreated from his eyes.

Heather glanced at Nathan for help. He nodded before scooting closer and raising his hands. The light swirled around his arms and poured into Aaron's wounds. All of us watched in fascination and horror.

"What did they do to you?" Disgust laced Ethan's voice.

"Nghh..." He wiggled around on the floor. "Lashes. Only lashes. They had other stuff prepared, but... that was all they did. Over, and over, and over."

Picturing him going through that put me through hell. He was the one who rescued me from that place, and in return, he got whipped. Damn it.

Theo's eyes burned with anger. "I swear. I'm gonna kill them. *All* of them."

Aaron let out a chuckle. "Save some for me."

"Deal."

All of us watched the light slowly close his deep wounds. His shallow breaths gradually became deeper and deeper.

We only had to hold out a couple more hours for whatever Aaron had planned next. No matter how scared I was to be tortured next, no matter how much I wanted to sulk over not being able to heal, I couldn't give up hope. I couldn't give up on Naomi. Not when her terror was the only thing keeping me moving.

CHAPTER

SEVENTEEN

"YOU HAVE BETRAYED HEAVEN AND ITS KIN!" LADY ELISHA hovered in the sky with Her wings spread out. "For that, you will fall."

Aaron crouched in the wreckage below. His wings were tattered with golden blood. The blessed sword stabbed through the ground in front of him.

He snarled. "You of all people... How dare you talk to me like that!"

He grabbed the sword and stood up, readying for battle.

"Would you like help, Lady Elisha?" an angel asked.

She raised Her hands. "I must do this on my own. Retreat to safety."

"As You wish."

Aaron and Lady Elisha stared at each other until everyone else flew out of sight. The silence was tense, furious, until he made his move.

He shot into the sky.

Elisha blinked before Her eyes glowed pure white. She swung

Her arm. Aaron blocked it with the blade. They pushed against one another, armor screeching against his steel.

Aaron raised his chin. "You will not deceive me any longer."

He slashed Her side, but She blocked the attack with Her arm. "I say the same to you, traitor."

She kicked, but Aaron blocked Her. She kicked again, Her foot a blur. Aaron plummeted toward the ground. He spread his wings to slow down his fall.

A laser shot toward him. He slashed it in half. When he landed, he flew back to meet Her.

Aaron swung the sword again and again, but She easily countered him. He struggled to get past Her defenses.

Soon, his wrathful frown turned into a grin. There was a malicious glint in his eyes before he disappeared.

She gasped.

This speed. It must've come from the Galactica.

She looked around. Even Her eyes couldn't keep up with him. She only caught wisps of him when he slowed down to attack. All She could do was block his senseless strikes.

His laughter grew louder and louder. He attacked harder, faster.

Blood.

Her body froze. Her glowing eyes turned back to their normal light blue hue. White blood dripped out of Her back and coughed from Her mouth. Her blood.

Searing pain. The pain of thousands of pins and needles stabbed Her at the same time and burned with the heat of powerful flames. But She wouldn't scream. She wouldn't give him the satisfaction.

Aaron sunk the blade deeper. Her pain-filled cry escaped for a moment despite Her efforts.

He laughed at Her scream.

Elisha never thought She could feel such pain. Not from anyone, and definitely not from Sarhiel.

~

"Caleb?" Someone shook my body. I heaved desperately for air.

"Caleb?"

My eyes burst open.

I pulled my arms to my chest and took in deep breaths, but I couldn't stop the terror inside.

Such murderous intent in Aaron's eyes. His laughter. It was so crude, so evil.

"Caleb." That voice. It was Nathan's voice. "It's time."

Our circumstances crashed toward me as I used the brick wall as a crutch and sat up. I could barely make out the rest of the group. The embers of the torches outside were dying down.

It reminded me of my cabin. I didn't have electricity, so I rarely had light unless I bothered to light the fireplace.

"How are we going to get out of here?" I asked, pushing the adrenaline down.

"Someone is going to come by and unlock the doors."

There was another voice. Not from the cell, or outside of it, but I knew I heard another voice.

"The hell?"

"I'm telepathic, Caleb. I can communicate through thoughts."

Right. Paul was a telepath. That vision of Aaron and Lady Elisha had messed with me more than I thought.

"Paul wasn't the only man I brought here." That whisper sent chills down my spine. Aaron was here. "There is another one posing as a guard."

How delirious was I? Of course Aaron would be here. But was the change still in effect? I didn't sense anything malevolent in his tone, but my fear cracked through my logic.

The man who'd stabbed Lady Elisha in the back was stuck in a cell with me. The one who slaughtered all those angels with that sickening laughter. The angel who betrayed everyone. And I didn't even know why he did it.

Footsteps approached us.

"Shut up, everyone," Theo hissed.

The footsteps stopped in front of our cell. An audible click was heard before they walked away. It had to be Aaron's other person.

"Your door is open. I'll give you directions," Paul said inside my head.

"Are we getting Gabriel first?" Theo asked.

"I would suggest meeting up with the other prisoners first. Strength in numbers."

Paul had a point. Even with the strength Gabriel's brother had, eight hundred people were not easy to beat for anyone. Then again, we had no idea how many Ravens were here. Still, we had a better shot with more people on our side. Despite my logic, my stomach ached at the thought of abandoning Gabriel.

"Paul's right," Aaron said. "Let's worry about Gabriel later. He can handle himself." Again, his tone wasn't nearly as cold as before. The change wasn't in effect after all.

Everyone stood behind the unlocked cell door and waited.

"You're clear. Go left and straight ahead. I'll tell you when any guards are close."

We walked out cautiously, looking for guards despite Paul's reassurance. But instead of following the others down the corridor, I walked straight to Paul's cell. I couldn't see him, but I knew he was inside.

"Are you coming with us?" It seemed wrong to leave him here.

"No," he answered aloud.

"But—"

"Go. I will be fine. I am meant to be here."

What? How was that supposed to make sense? It would be wrong to leave him here. I would never be able to face Naomi again if I left *anyone* here.

"Hey." Everyone stopped and looked at me when I spoke. "Does anyone have a pin or a needle?"

"No," Ethan answered. "Why?"

Picking the lock was all I could think of. "I have to help him."

"Go away. I don't need rescuing," Paul said.

"No. I'm not leaving another Swan be—"

Suddenly, I was dragged away from Paul's cell. I tried breaking from their grip, but it was too strong.

"Hey! We can't just leave him there." There was finally something I could do to help, and they were stopping me.

We halted when a hidden door opened in the wall. Then we stepped through it, that same hard grip pulling me along. The wall closed behind us.

"No!"

My hand was finally released. By *Aaron*.

His eyebrows furrowed. "We're supposed to be on a *team*, Caleb."

"I couldn't just leave him there."

"Don't yell, you *idiot*," Aaron growled.

"So I'm an idiot now?"

Heather approached us with her hands up. "Come on, Caleb. Calm down."

I huffed, anguish crashing into my anger. Aaron was the one who killed Lady Elisha. What was I supposed to think about him with that image playing over and over in my head? "Heather, I—"

"Besides," Aaron interrupted. My eyes darted to him. He seemed calmer than he was in my dream, even through his small frown showing his earlier anger. He wasn't the same person. Not right now, anyway. "I already asked him if he wanted to leave. He wanted to stay."

I looked to the floor. That was what Paul had said back there. Why would he want to stay, though? To keep giving Aaron intel perhaps?

My teeth dug into my bottom lip as I nodded, dropping the argument, but my harsh emotions still remained. It felt wrong to leave him in such an awful place.

We started walking again straight through the corridor. Multiple side-tunnels connected off our path, filled with countless cells and chambers. It seemed endless.

"Stop."

We froze.

"There's a guard around that corner. On your right."

All of us stuck against the wall as we waited for the all-clear. The tension inside me burned. Gabriel could've handled himself for a while longer, right?

"Go."

We darted silently across.

"Now go left."

We did. This tunnel wasn't filled with cells like the others, and the torches were much brighter here. We had to be more careful of guards lurking around.

My ears twitched when I heard breathing on the other side of the wall to my right. The others didn't seem to acknowledge it, if they noticed.

We almost reached the end of the hall when I noticed the only way we could turn was right.

"Everyone is in a room to your right," Paul said. *"I've told them to be quiet. Please try to keep it that way."* That explained the breathing I heard.

We turned the corner and the tunnel opened up into a huge, square room. The ceiling was low enough to touch, but it was big enough to house the gigantic crowd that stood inside it.

It was obvious that they were the prisoners: from their grime-filled, ragged clothes to their skinny, gaunt frames. My desire to save such a pitiful looking group grew in their presence.

They whispered under their breaths. Some of them mentioned their doubts while others pressed on how long they had been waiting for their revenge. I could've only imagined what they went through here. I got a sneak-peak when Aaron returned after his bruising, and it wasn't pretty.

Suddenly, they stopped talking and turned to us with expressionless faces.

"I told them you were here."

Even though they only spoke in faint whispers before, the sudden silence made me freeze. Luckily, I wasn't being stared at alone.

We stepped further into the room and towards the center of the wall next to us. I studied Aaron closely, anxiously wondering if he would change again.

We stopped.

"Is everyone ready?" Aaron said.

Everyone looked at each other, exchanging glances in the crowd, and nodded.

"Then follow me." Aaron raised his hand with a grin. "Today, Raven blood will spill."

Instead of shouting in response, the prisoners raised their hands with closed fists, imitating Aaron's gesture. Some of them smiled, some of them frowned, but all of them had the same determined look in their eyes.

After lowering their arms, everyone followed us back into the tunnels. Hundreds of footsteps clanged loudly in the stone labyrinth, but there was no point in being super sneaky now. We had an army. Still, an army was not what I was hoping to find here. Had I come for nothing after all?

CHAPTER

EIGHTEEN

It surprised me that no one had spotted us yet. Then again, the crowd's steps were surprisingly quiet. It was probably out of habit from being held captive here and trying not to draw attention to themselves.

Our group had split up in order to cover the crowd's back and front. Theo, Nathan and I walked behind them, while Aaron, Ethan, and Heather led the front.

My desire to help outweighed the relief I had knowing that that gun was nowhere near me. Theo and Nathan walked with tense arms, ready for a fight, and I couldn't even heal. My memories had better be here, for Naomi's sake.

"Hey!" someone shouted. We froze. I heard footsteps running towards us from an intersecting tunnel ahead. "Stop!" It was a guard, but it was only one from what I could decipher.

After a couple blows I couldn't see, Paul told me, *"Sorry about that. I didn't think one guard could do much against a couple hundred people anyway. Looks like I was right."*

Not even a warning? What an obtuse jackass.

Theo crossed his arms and pouted. "I didn't even get to do anything."

Nathan giggled at his comment and Theo's eyes darted away from him. Strange, but I didn't have time to figure out what was going on between them. I had Naomi and Gabriel on my mind. I shivered.

We continued our trek through the infinite halls, Paul guiding us to an exit. Just when I thought everyone would escape—just when I thought I had come here for nothing—a huge explosion erupted in front of the crowd. There was definitely more than one guard up there.

"Sarhiel!" That sounded like Gabriel. No, it was his brother. Shit.

"We're trapped," Nathan said.

I turned around. Guards charged toward us with hateful cries.

"Fuck." I instinctively reached for my holster. It was empty. All I could do was watch.

The Ravens' fists sparkled with light. Nathan turned to his side as a shield of light formed around his arm. Theo sighed before reluctantly doing the same thing, blocking the tunnel.

I stepped back. Every part of my body trembled—my arms, my legs, my lungs. The crowd behind me screamed in terror and rage. The sounds of battle crashed ahead, but I couldn't turn around to see the blows.

The Ravens pounded on their shields. They dug their heels in. Even so, they squeezed against the crowd, until their shields were inches from my face.

"Quick! There's a hidden door on the wall to your left. Hurry!"

I dashed to the wall, pushing against the crowd. I hammered against the rough bricks.

Hurry.

A battle-cry burst from Theo's lips. I turned my head towards them, my intuition knowing that whatever happened to instigate that cry wasn't good. Their shields had been broken.

I gritted my teeth and shoved the wall. Bricks smashed onto the floor, revealing another tunnel lined with empty cells. If there were any guards, they were nowhere in sight.

But this couldn't have been a secret door. If it was, the bricks wouldn't be rubble on the ground. But this wasn't the time to analyze it.

"Come on!" I yelled.

The crowd sprinted to the opening, pushing me against the wall. But some remained.

I made eye contact with one. A woman slightly taller than me, with fierce brown eyes and red locks that hadn't been washed in weeks. "We aren't leaving you!"

I opened my mouth to object, but nothing came out. How could they be so brave?

The hundred or so that didn't run bolted toward the Ravens. Flashes of light crashed against each other.

"This is *awesome*," Theo shouted against the onslaught. Now really wasn't the time...

The last few prisoners had slipped into the tunnel, leaving more space behind them. I could finally see what was happening up ahead, where Gabriel's brother had attacked.

Some prisoners had stayed to fight there, too, but only around half of them were still standing. The rest lay on the ground, bloodied and bruised. Heather desperately tried to heal them, as Ethan fought off the wave of Ravens, while Aaron occupied Gabriel's brother.

Aaron threw a punch, but the Raven blocked it easily and elbowed him, pushing Aaron back.

"Where are they?" Aaron said.

"What are you talking about?" he answered in a mocking tone.

"Caleb's memories. And Gabriel. Tell me where they are!"

I slowly walked closer to them, my curiosity urging me on despite my fear. Naomi and Gabriel. I had to save them both.

Gabriel's brother laughed. "Why would you care? All you are is a backstabber."

He aimed a punch at Aaron's chin. As Aaron blocked, the Raven opened his fist and a bang of light exploded from his palm. Aaron was blinded as the Raven kicked him into the wall.

Wind blasted through my hair. Despite the intense impact, the wall was only slightly damaged, red blood decorating the dents.

Aaron slumped over, forcing his fists to stay in front of his cheeks. "Like you're one to talk, Leo."

Leo grunted, raising his chin, before hoisting his arms above his head with interlocked, glowing hands. There was nothing I could do. He slammed his fists toward Aaron's head. A whip of light struck the Raven's arms, throwing him off balance. His balance faltered only for a moment, but it was long enough.

Aaron's whips of light hung down from his arms. Blood trailed from his mouth. His lips raised into a familiar grin. *Oh, no.*

"Fine, then." His hardened green eyes shot up to meet Leo's. "I've been waiting to kill someone anyway."

Leo's stance widened. Although I couldn't see his expression, I felt the newfound tension emanating from them.

Aaron changed.

Leo vanished. Light beamed from Aaron before whips shot out around him. Aaron bashed the entire tunnel with no care or thought at all.

The Ravens surrounding us were forced to back off. The prisoners, along with Nathan and Theo, ran to the opening I made for cover. I tried to follow them, but the whips blocked my path.

One grazed my nose. Another smashed into my foot before I could dodge it. But the stinging, throbbing pain was nothing compared to the shocked look on Heather's face.

Everyone shared that look, but she wasn't moving for cover.

She wouldn't leave the injured behind. And Ethan had stayed with her, shouting at her to move, but her stubbornness got in the way.

Damn it.

I ran towards her.

"Don't do it! Get to cover now!"

I ignored Paul's warning along with my own doubts and kept running.

One whip rocked toward my face. I dived lower, keeping my momentum. I wouldn't stop. Another crashed towards my legs. I hopped over it as another bolted toward me midair. There was no escape. I swung backwards, the whip barely whizzing past me as I fell onto my back. Air heaved from my chest before one smashed into my face. My nose throbbed with an indescribable pain. Iron seeped into my nostrils, but I had to keep pressing on.

I shot onto my soles and ran. I was so close now.

My feet jumped over another whip, reaching out towards Heather, above the injured that she cared for. She stared at me with pure terror and disbelief in her eyes.

"Caleb! Look out!"

She pointed behind me. When my eyes followed where her finger aimed, there wasn't another whip. It was Leo. His finger grazed my ankle, and suddenly, I smelled something other than blood. I smelled... flowers.

I sat on the curb of the cobblestone road. The bustling city felt much too crowded. The only reason I liked this part of Heaven was because Naomi lived here.

I smiled at the thought of her. I'd only met her a year ago, and we were already close friends.

I wasn't supposed to meet her today. I just liked sitting on the street near her house. It sounded strange to think that, like I was stalking her. Was I?

"Caleb!"

My eyes widened. I looked up and there she was, running towards me. I grinned, but she didn't smile back. In fact, she looked worried. My brows twinged as I stood up.

She braked and handed something to me. It was a flower, but not an ordinary one. It was the one I'd given her a couple months ago. But it had become wilted and deformed. My heart filled with sadness at the sight.

"I'm sorry, Caleb," she said. "The flower. It—"

It wasn't dead yet. That was good. It just became ill.

I closed my eyes. A slight breeze passed through the street. I caught it and spun the energy around my body. First, it brought chills, then a warmth surrounded me.

The light circled around my arms. I concentrated the energy into my palm and up the stem of the flower. I felt the flower's hope as it grasped onto the energy.

When I opened my eyes, the flower was more than restored. The dark purple petals had grown, and the golden stem shone brighter.

Naomi's eyes burst with wonder. She tried to say something, but it came out as a weird, gargled sound.

I grinned. "Someday, I'm going to help angels. I'll be a healer separate from the Sanandum."

I gave the flower back. Her eyes locked onto me. "I can't wait to see it."

I WALKED around the crystal-clear lake surrounded by miles upon miles of forest. Even though there were others around, the air and the waves were refreshing. It wasn't nearly as crowded as the city.

My ankle stung. I looked down, but I didn't see a cut. Soon, an unfamiliar face appeared with the pain. I scanned the area until I found the kid who'd gotten hurt.

I approached him and a woman. The kid analyzed a cut on his ankle with a pout. They were close to shore. He probably cut it on some rocks.

"You'll be fine. It'll heal in a couple minutes," the woman said.

"But it hurts really bad," the kid whined.

"Hey." I waved at them. "I can heal it for you if you want."

"Really?" the kid asked.

I nodded and crouched down. He put his foot in front of me. My hand hovered over the cut for a second before I pulled it away and the tiny wound was gone.

The kid grinned. "Thank you!"

I smiled. "Happy to help."

I LOVED THE TREES. They provided great shade, looked amazing, and were always happy to let you sit by them.

It sounded childish, but it was true. I'd always preferred plants over people. Naomi was the exception, of course.

But right now, my feelings toward her were mixed. Did she really join without anyone else convincing her? Vax or Leo must've gotten into her head somehow.

"I thought I'd find you here."

She stood at my side, gazing at me. I wanted to smile, but this feeling of betrayal wouldn't go away.

I glanced away. In the corner of my eye, she sat down next to me. She adjusted her dress, eyes darting awkwardly away for a second, then whipped her head towards me.

"Are you mad at me?"

"No. Just... You surprised me."

She released a long sigh. "I know. But I'm not a healer like you. I'm a fighter."

Naomi. A fighter. It was hard to understand, but easy at the same time.

"Besides, the Pugnare hasn't been in combat for a long time."

Right. She meant not in a war for a long time. They'd had to deal with plenty of sinning angels over the years.

"I don't want you to get hurt." I placed my forehead on my palm and leaned into my hand. "I don't want anyone to get hurt."

Naomi's head popped up, her smile blossoming with enthusiasm. "Then how about you join the Sanandum?"

We'd had this conversation before. If only she understood. The Sanandum supported conflict. They only healed people so they could fight.

I turned to her and begged, pleaded, with my eyes. Could she really be asking me to take part in such a thing?

"Naomi..."

"Why not? You're one of the best healers I've ever seen. The Sanandum needs someone like you." She leaned closer. "You're special, Caleb."

I looked at the meadow in front of me and the trees circling it.

"It would only further conflict. Besides." I glanced at her. "I'm content just being your soulmate."

Confusion blasted onto her face. "But don't you like helping people? You've already been healing people around town whenever they ask. Why would this be any different?"

"I—" That sickening, awful feeling came back again. I didn't want to be anywhere near the Guards' base. That was too close to the Gods' castle. Too close to Him. "I do like helping people."

"Then how about you try it?"

I put some distance between us, her words making me nauseated.

"Please?"

She didn't understand. No one.else understood, either. Not my parents, not anyone who noticed my talent. Nobody.

"We need you, Caleb," she said.

I knew my talents would go a long way in the Sanandum, but healing people just to fight seemed wrong to me. The cycle was endless and destructive.

"You could always resign when wars start," she reasoned. "You'd just be someone who helped whenever training accidents happen."

I gazed at the ground. Maybe... that didn't sound so bad. Like she said before, that was what I'd been doing with most of my time anyway.

"Okay." I reluctantly nodded and looked into her eyes. "Fine. I'll do it."

She smiled. "Thank you."

My MEMORIES. I got some of them back.

Leo's golden eyes brimmed with determination. His hand almost wrapped around my foot before a whip slashed between us, forcing him back and making him disappear again.

I fell over a bloodied body, everyone's throbbing pain making me sloppy. They groaned in response. I winced and quickly muttered an apology before scooting off them, crouching next to Heather.

"Caleb! Go get cover," she yelled, whips flying around us.

"I won't leave you guys."

Ethan, who stood above Heather with a shield, gestured his arms toward me. "Not you, too." He blocked a whip crashing from above.

I snatched Heather's hand.

"What are you doing?" she asked with a confused scowl.

"The only thing that'll get you to move!"

Her eyes twitched in realization before I closed my eyes. I had heard of angels combining their energy to heal, but I'd never actually attempted it before. Hopefully it wasn't too hard.

A whip slashed into my side.

These whips would make this hard, but dealing with everyone's pain all at once was a much bigger struggle. My entire body felt covered in bruises. Some Swans even had lacerations digging into their skin. And a few of them were already dead.

I tightened my jaw and let the energy flow. The light swirled around Heather and I almost effortlessly and shot into the wounded. The strangest part was feeling a foreign energy under my control. More than a few times, it almost rushed back to Heather, but with her command, it spun back into the wounded.

With one final push of energy, I opened my eyes. The people still alive sluggishly stood up before sticking to the walls, avoiding Aaron's whips.

They were okay. I did it.

I turned to Heather. She smiled at me, and for a moment, there was relief.

"You got your memories back." Ethan gawked from above. His eyes switched to something over my shoulder before he dashed toward it, blocking a whip and pushing into my back.

I peeked around him. The hole in the wall was far, but it wasn't impossible to reach. Especially now that some of the escapees spawned shields of light covering their comrades.

Heather and I stood. "Let's go," I said, sounding more confident than I was.

We dashed toward the hole, whips bashing against the shields. Some of the whips were too fast, and I felt the fallen angels' bones crack, felt their skin sting. But we slipped through.

The rest of the prisoners that had gone in before us hadn't

gone far. From what they said, they had stayed out of concern for us. That was somewhat comforting.

Nathan scowled at Theo, holding his hand. Theo tried to wriggle out of his grip to no avail. "But I can't just stand back and watch," Theo barked.

Nathan noticed us first. The color returned to his face as the corners of his lips slightly rose.

Theo whipped around and saw us, flinching with surprise. "You guys are okay."

Nathan swiped his hand back to his side as Theo ran towards the three of us. He hugged all of us at once. "I'm so happy you guys aren't dead."

We only had a second to breathe before the cracks of Aaron's whips sent tremors through the ground. Theo pulled away as we stared at the strips of light as they became unrecognizable blurs.

A poisonous cackle echoed around the chamber—one that I hadn't heard since that dream. Aaron's booming laugh was tinged with madness, giving me skin-crawling shivers, just like what I felt from Naomi.

"Sarhiel! Stop this madness!" Leo shouted among the slams and the howls of laughter. Aaron didn't answer. He kept laughing hysterically, continuing his chaotic bombardment.

"We can't leave him here," I said. No matter how reckless he was right now, he was only trying to save us.

"I know," Heather responded.

Ethan looked behind us. "But what about the prisoners? And Gabriel?"

Those were the exact questions rushing through my mind.

"We'll split up," Nathan said, stepping closer to us. "It should be easier for the crowd now that Aaron took out a chunk of the guards."

Being separated didn't sound great, but it was the best option we had to save everyone, so I nodded.

"I'm staying," Heather said.

I narrowed my eyes. "Me too."

"Okay."

Nathan eyed Ethan and Theo. Ethan bowed his head without complaint, but Theo crossed his arms. "The action is just starting to get good around here."

Nathan cocked his head with a grimace.

Theo waved his hand at the crowd. "It's not like they're *totally* defenseless. Some of them are fighters. Right, guys?"

A good chunk of them raised their hands with glowing palms.

"See?"

"Fine," Nathan spat. He waved Ethan over before running to the crowd. Ethan followed him after giving us a reassuring nod. After a couple shouts, they ran off with the prisoners, leaving us alone with Aaron and Leo. My body relaxed as the injured got farther and farther away.

"How are we doing this?" Theo asked. It must've been bad if Theo of all people didn't just rush in there.

"I don't know," I thought out loud.

Pain exploded inside me. My legs buckled, but I leaned against the wall for support before falling completely to my knees.

"Caleb!" they yelled.

"Are you all right?" Heather asked.

I bit my lip. "Yeah. Yeah, I'm fine."

Leo.

I looked up, and their eyes followed mine. Leo shakily stood up not too far from Aaron. Cuts decorated his body like painted strips. Although he handled the pain well, I knew what he felt. His skin stung with a throbbing pain, and the sharp cuts only intensified it. One of his ribs was definitely fractured.

Was Aaron this powerful all along? To be on par with someone who could move faster than the eye could see was completely insane.

Aaron raised his arms. "I'm gonna kill you all!"

Yes, that was what he was. Completely insane.

The whips snapped faster. Faster.

Leo grunted before disappearing out of view. I heard him yell retreat, and felt the deep, piercing pain in his chest, and then, he and the few Ravens left were out of sight.

"Huh?" Aaron stared at the Ravens fleeing for their lives with a scowl that deepened every second. "Come back here!" He charged at them full speed.

With Leo's pain farther away, I was able to stand, but I wasn't fast enough to stop Heather from running after him.

"Heather, no!" I screamed.

Theo followed her, a shield appearing on his arm. Theo was forced to stop and block Aaron's whips more than once, but Heather darted through them. It looked as if a certain tunnel vision overtook her as her legs weaved through his barrage. Theo was far behind her by the time Heather reached out her hand to Aaron.

"Aaron, stop!"

Aaron swung around, his eyes drenched in rage. His palm swung toward her jaw until his eyes widened. The whips stopped, gently floating in midair.

I carefully stepped into the hall, limping from the remnants of pain around us. The Ravens had long disappeared, except for the corpses lying on the ground.

Aaron's hand froze next to Heather's cheek. He huffed until the rage in his eyes diminished, his lips lowering into a thoughtful frown. His hand dragged gently against her cheek. "Heather..."

They weren't soulmates my *ass*.

I lowered my head as my thoughts deepened from that snarky remark. My longing for Naomi's touch, for her skin against mine, had grown each day I woke up without her.

I glanced up as Aaron's whips broke into sparks of light, before falling like snow and fading away. His hand remained on her cheek. He stared at her with a soft expression. Although Heather's expression was hidden from my view, her body had noticeably relaxed at his touch.

"Get a room, you two! Before you play some backseat bingo," Theo teased. So even a dunderhead like Theo could pick up on their hints.

Aaron reacted slowly, pulling his arm back to his side and looking at Theo and me. Heather spun around with a spiteful stare. "Why can't you shut up for once?"

Theo let out a quick chuckle.

"We should go," I said, not knowing what else to say.

Aaron nodded before running for the makeshift hole. The three of us watched him closely before trailing behind.

It had only taken us a couple minutes to catch up with the rest of the Swans, and Paul had guided us to a new exit that the front of the crowd had just reached. Despite the show of power we had faced, this mission seemed to be a success. That didn't mean I wasn't weary of every shadow and corner. Leo was still alive, just wounded. It wouldn't take long to heal him and all the other surviving Ravens.

"Why are they going so slow?" Theo complained.

"'Cause not a lot of people can climb up at the same time, dumbass," Ethan answered. While Ethan was behind the swarm with us, Nathan had led them.

"What are we going to do about Gabriel after the prisoners leave?" I asked.

Even though the prisoners' whispers had been quiet, somehow, the silence around me exploded.

Aaron looked away before turning back to me. "It's too risky to stay longer than we need to," he said. "We need to leave with them."

My mouth dropped. "What?"

"There's no way we're leaving him behind," Theo said. "Not when Aaron can fuck Leo up."

Heather hushed him before Aaron explained. "I don't want to do that when it's not necessary. You saw the way I acted back there."

Theo dramatically waved his arms. "What do you mean by *not necessary?* Gabriel's gone!"

"Theo's right." It was hard to believe that I'd just said that. "We can't leave him here."

"Exactly," Ethan agreed.

"But with Leo here, how would we find him in time?" Heather reasoned, gesturing to the crowd. "We still have all of these people to worry about."

I stepped forward. "But—"

"We have to get them to safety, or this mission fails," Aaron stated. I stared at him a while longer, trying to conjure up some reason he was wrong, but I couldn't.

"Fine," I spat.

Not another word was spoken, but their faces said it all. Theo scowled with growing impatience. Ethan gazed into the distance with sadness in his eyes. Heather's expression held that same sad glint. Aaron... Aaron was closed off completely. I could tell he was deep in thought, but I had no clues as to what he felt. Hopefully, Gabriel could hold out a little while longer.

I climbed out through the trapdoor and into the forest above. What was with fallen angels and building stuff underground?

Everyone else had already gotten out—and without another incident, surprisingly.

We were incredibly lucky that Leo hadn't come after us yet, and I knew we had to get the recently freed prisoners to safety, but my body didn't move from next to the trapdoor.

My friends surrounded me. Heather analyzed me especially closely, like she knew what I was about to say.

"We need to go back now," I said. "They can take care of themselves."

Heather gestured to the crowd with her palm. "We can't just abandon them, Caleb. You know what they went through."

My brows sank. She wouldn't change her mind. "Fine." I turned back to the trapdoor alone and—

"Gabriel isn't there anymore."

Paul's voice froze me in my tracks.

"What?" I asked out loud, my voice trembling. He couldn't be dead. The guy that helped me gain confidence in this world couldn't be dead.

"Don't worry. He's alive," Paul said. *"But you need to go. All of you."*

I swung back around. All of their faces emanated their shock, including the mysterious Aaron. But he recovered notably quickly. "We can't let our efforts be wasted. *Including* Gabriel's," he said.

I nibbled on my cheek, thinking about what the right thing to do was. Gabriel was able to move as fast as Leo. No one else here could do that—unless one counted Aaron's alter ego—including the prisoners we freed. They wouldn't be free long if we didn't lead them to the Owl tunnels.

Nathan walked toward me and grabbed my bicep. "Let's do this."

I shivered, Naomi's terror grating my mind. If Nathan noticed, he didn't acknowledge it.

"Okay," I said, a huge pit remaining in my stomach.

CHAPTER

NINETEEN

WE SPRINTED THROUGH THE PINE FOREST TO LEAD THE crowd, not bothering to cover our tracks. There was no time. Paul had been leading us to the Owl tunnels ever since we took off. We also had been sporadically healing the wounded prisoners, but even then, we didn't stop.

Gabriel and Naomi sucked me into my thoughts more than once. Naomi was in danger. I constantly felt it in my stomach and at the edge of my mind. And now, Gabriel had been captured, and by his brother no less.

I didn't remember much about Leo from my own memories, but from what I gathered, he was powerful. Gabriel was strong too, but how long could he last against his equal?

"The entrance is just up ahead," Paul said.

We approached the base of a mountain towering above us. Stone and dirt stacked on top of each other to create the majestic sight.

We stopped.

Aaron stepped closer and rubbed his hand against the hard dirt before turning to face the crowd. "This is where we leave you," he yelled. "I hope you guys can live your lives free from the Ravens' shackles."

Wait, what? Why wouldn't we go through the Owl tunnels, too? It would be much less risky than taking the cars back.

The former prisoners exchanged glances before one person blurted out, "But we can't leave without returning the favor."

"Yeah," someone else shouted. "It wouldn't be right."

Aaron smiled warmly. "I might take up your offer one day. But right now, just stay safe."

Their eyes rounded with shock before they murmured countless things. Still, no one else objected. It was strange to think that Aaron rampaged with a gnawing hunger for blood earlier today.

The dirt on the mountain broke apart before clumping on the sides of a deep tunnel lined with lights.

Aaron stepped back, along with the rest of us. Loud footsteps stomped toward the entrance. A huge, bulky man sprinted toward us at blazing speed. He must've been an Owl.

As he got closer, I noticed a tattoo circling his shoulder and peeking out from his chest under his tank top. He was just as tall, if not taller, than Gabriel. I swallowed my fear. Even though he looked intimidating, he was here to help.

He slowed down and walked out of the tunnel, surveyed the crowd, and stepped out of the way. "Follow the tunnel. There are others down here that can help you find your way."

Everyone cautiously walked through the tunnel. Everyone but us.

"Why aren't we going with them?" I turned to Nathan, the closest person to me.

His eyes shot to the ground as he rubbed his wrist. He had his sister's nervous habit. That wasn't a good sign.

Ethan's explanation of the Owl tunnels came back to me. *They let people from any faction in, as long as they don't get violent.*

My eyes widened. Of course.

I looked across the tunnel where Heather and Aaron stood. I saw glimpses of Aaron as the crowd marched into the tunnel, but he didn't seem to notice me. He was too busy looking at the Owl before him.

The Owl crossed his arms. "We have the prisoners now, so scram."

Aaron was the reason we couldn't go in.

"I heard that Aaron was an Owl before," Theo explained. "I don't know what he did, but he did something violent and got kicked out." He shrugged in the corner of my eye. "Owls just sound like a bunch of poltroons to me."

Ethan shot him a dirty look, but I was desensitized to Theo's quick quips by now. I was too busy wondering what Aaron had done.

"I'll stay until all of them get inside," Aaron said. "I promise, I won't step foot in there."

The Owl grunted, but didn't say anything else.

What had he done? That question remained in my mind until the last of the prisoners walked into the tunnel. Now, I had a clear view of Aaron and Heather, along with the huge Owl.

I walked toward them, the others following me.

"I'm surprised he hasn't stabbed you in the back yet, Heather. But he'll do it sooner or later," the Owl said.

"No, he won't. He's changed, Orion."

The Owl, named Orion apparently, rolled his eyes.

Aaron finally noticed me. Shame sheened in his irises.

"What did you do?" I asked him calmly, my curiosity overtaking my senses.

Heather gasped an offended breath and was about to speak for him when Aaron put his hand on her shoulder. Her head spun toward his before she took a deep, calming breath. Aaron slid his hand back down to his side.

"I was an Owl before, but my condition was much worse back

then. And even after telling them what was wrong with me, they accepted me. Orion and a couple others even tried to cure me, but I... I went rogue on a mission."

"More like massacred half of our squad," Orion spitefully added.

Aaron sighed and rubbed his neck. "Yeah."

He killed half of his own squad? But he had stopped himself from hurting Heather back there. Although, he did say his condition was worse back then.

"I'm sorry I didn't tell you back at the base. I was just... I still *am* ashamed of it."

Lady Elisha's last screams as Aaron plunged the sword into Her back echoed in my head. Ever since that dream, whenever I pictured Aaron, I saw an insane killer thirsty for blood. But after what I saw in the Tenebris, when he stopped himself from hurting Heather...

My brows burrowed into my nose. "If you *weren't* ashamed of that, you'd be a terrible person."

His droopy brows spiked up in astonishment. I playfully slapped his arm. "Swans stick together."

His stare didn't fade. Whatever answer he expected, I knew mine wasn't one of them. I couldn't blame him for being surprised. If I hadn't seen him stop himself in the Tenebris, I might've sided with the Owl. But I had seen it.

"Oh yeah!" Theo punched me in the shoulder, much harder than I patted Aaron's. "Does this mean you're a Swan now?"

I flung out my arms. "I think so."

Theo jumped in celebration.

"It's been obvious for a while now," Ethan said with a smile.

"It has," Heather agreed. "But I'm glad you said it."

"Me too," Nathan murmured.

Aaron let out an exasperated laugh. "I don't believe it. You've looked past so many things I've done." He gestured to everyone in the group. "All of you have."

"Me neither." The Owl walked back into the tunnel. "Just be careful," he muttered under his breath before the tunnel closed again. For someone who hated Aaron, those last few words were far too heartfelt.

"Let's head back to the cars before our luck runs out," Ethan suggested.

Everyone nodded.

CHAPTER

TWENTY

We darted back to the cars, making sure not to run into the Tenebris. Paul helped us out with that by giving us some much-needed directions.

Through the relief and pride I felt that we successfully freed the prisoners and retrieved some of my memories, was a deep, deep pain. Gabriel was taken, and all we knew was what Paul had told us. *He isn't there anymore.*

Where had Leo taken him? And why?

I wasn't any less worried about Naomi, either. Her shivering terror being a constant made it easy to become accustomed to, but that didn't mean the emotion disappeared.

"I think I see one of them," Ethan said.

I looked ahead and saw it, too—the brown car that Aaron, Theo, Nathan, and I rode here in. I was surprised that it was still there and not destroyed by the Ravens. Hell, I was surprised Leo hadn't come after us yet. Goosebumps crawled on my back at the thought of him.

We stopped next to the car. Aaron put his hand on the roof. "We'll do the same arrangements as before to drive back to base."

"What about Gabriel?" I asked.

"Leo took him to the Subplicium," Paul said on cue.

Theo dragged his eyelids down his cheek with his fingers. "No way." From the shocked looks on his and everyone else's faces, that place was bad news.

"Are you sure?" Heather asked out loud.

"Yes," Paul said. *"If Leo didn't care about ceremony, he would've executed Gabriel the day you got captured."*

Dizziness swarmed around me all because of that one word. *Executed.*

"He's going to execute him?" I asked, my voice trembling.

Nathan stepped beside me. "Gabriel's strong. Trust him."

"But we don't even know where this place is, do we?"

"The sooner we get back, the sooner we can find it," Heather added.

Was that all we could do? Run back and hide like scared rabbits?

I gnawed impatiently on the inside of my cheek. Gabriel had to hold out a little longer. "Then let's hurry."

They nodded.

"Let's go, Heather," Ethan said before they ran off to search for the other car.

The rest of us got inside as Aaron turned on the engine. "Buckle up."

CHAPTER
TWENTY-ONE

I spotted Gabriel on the balcony and walked to the white railings. Almost everything was either white or red in the Pugnare's section of the castle.

Gabriel didn't acknowledge me as I approached him, so I looked out onto the courtyard. Trees adorned the corners and flowers lined the perimeter.

"Why did you want to meet me, Gabriel?" I asked, the silence begging me to.

"I just wanted to tell you that I'm really honored to have you with the Sanandum." He looked at me with a grin.

"Thanks," I said. "But that's not the reason I joined."

"Oh?" Gabriel raised a brow. "Does it have anything to do with a soulmate, by chance?"

My lips curved up. "It was everything to do with one."

He chuckled and leaned on the rails. "I remember my soulmate. He was everything to me."

I looked at the sky. The clouds were beautiful today, puffy like always.

"Soulmates make angels like us complete," Gabriel said. "But don't let the link consume you."

My brow twitched in surprise. "Why would you say that?"

His smile deteriated along with the shine in his golden eyes. "Let's just say I've seen some things. Strange things."

My eyes narrowed. Why would he bring up such a dark topic? An angel being corrupted by his own soulmate. It was something that hadn't happened in tens of thousands of years—something that only the oldest angels ever saw.

"Naomi wouldn't do that to me."

The air around us turned stagnant. The wind that had blown through moments ago vanished. Even the air didn't want to be a part of this conversation.

Gabriel beamed that trademark smile and the wind returned. "Very well," he said in his usual cheery voice. "I trust your judgment."

He patted my shoulder before walking away. I watched him in utter confusion.

So DARK. I could barely see anything beyond the haze. Someone held me by the shoulders. He shook me as he spoke.

"Listen to me, Caleb." His voice. Gabriel. I needed to focus to hear him. Focus. "You can't tell anyone what I'm about to do."

He was going to stop Anacora, stop His manipulation. I wanted to smile, but gravity was so heavy. Everything was so heavy.

Gabriel didn't take his hands away, but I couldn't feel anything anymore. Numbness coated every inch of my body like it was a sensation of its own.

"I don't think I can do that," I said.

His eyes spiked open. He shook me so much it made me dizzy. "Snap out of it, Caleb!" He repeated my name at the top of his lungs *over and over. His voice slowly sounded more and more distant. Until it was gone.*

~

IT WAS dark and ice cold. Of course, it was. It was nighttime. The shining moon above me offered proof.

My head buzzed. I sat on my knees in the castle. The Gods' castle. A boy was in front of me. All I saw was the shadow of His figure and wings, but I knew who He was.

My head buzzed louder. My body was so heavy. I couldn't get up. Why couldn't I get up?

"Tell me." The boy's voice was darker than any angel's voice should've been. Silky smooth and evil. "What has Gabriel been up to?"

The buzzing faded away, but the heaviness remained. I couldn't move, but I needed to escape. I had to get out of here.

I opened my mouth. No. A force opened my mouth, and my voice came out.

"He has been plotting against you." No! Take it back. Gabriel told me to keep it a secret. He trusted me. No, he deserved this. "My Lord." Yes. Gabriel deserved it.

The boy started laughing. His voice sounded so much sweeter than before. But wasn't His voice always this sweet?

~

I JOLTED AWAKE. The car was too confining, too restricting. I had to get out of here. I had to leave.

Nathan grabbed my hand, like the last time I freaked out around him. But this time he didn't say a word. He merely waited. His comforting stare reminded me to breathe.

I followed his silent command and took in a couple, deep

breaths. That helped considerably, but the anxiety didn't fully dissipate. Not after what I'd seen.

I should've been used to nightmares by now, but no matter how many I had, I always had the same adverse reaction.

"Geez, you're gonna give me a heart attack," Theo snarked, glancing back at me through the rearview mirror, but I barely paid attention to him.

I was the one who'd given Gabriel up to Anacora. *I* was the reason he fell. If I hadn't betrayed him, Gabriel wouldn't be captured and on his way to be executed. This was all *my* fault.

Aaron turned around from the passenger seat. I had woken him up, too. How loud had I been?

"Are you all right, Caleb?" he asked.

Nathan dropped my hand, but he looked at me with that same concerned look that Aaron did. I imagined their concern turning into horror and disgust, with piercing scowls and betrayed eyes.

"I'm fine," I said. "It was only a bad dream."

Aaron gave me a small, sad smile. "Well, try to get some sleep if you can," he said before rotating back into his sleeping position.

Nathan popped another quick smile before settling into his seat and closing his eyes.

Thank goodness. They bought it. I would tell them what I really saw eventually. I just couldn't bear to see those looks on their faces yet.

Theo snickered. "Yeah. Welcome to my world."

I shook my head and let out an annoyed groan as I leaned back into my seat. I probably wouldn't get back to sleep for a while, but I could at least try. Tomorrow we would be back at base, and we would finally formulate our plan. And hopefully, we wouldn't be too late.

CHAPTER

TWENTY-TWO

I closed the car door and stretched my arms. Being in that car for almost a whole day made my body stiff. It made my mind stiff, too, thinking about Gabriel all that time.

Aaron, Theo, and Nathan walked toward the hidden trapdoor. I followed them and noticed the other car close by, empty.

We stopped after only a couple steps. All I saw below us was grass, but Aaron reached down and opened the trapdoor without having to search at all.

The lights below were already on. The others were must've been down there.

"Go ahead," Aaron said to both of us.

I let Nathan and Theo climb down first, then I trailed behind. When my feet touched the metal floor, a strange sensation hit me. This long, almost never-ending hallway was the same one Heather had carried me through when the Ravens attacked. That seemed so long ago.

"We should wash up," Theo muttered.

I nodded.

The trapdoor closed, and Aaron descended after us.

It felt wrong to even think about having a shower with Gabriel missing. Still, there was nothing else I could do. There was nothing *any* of us could do.

WATER RAINED ONTO MY HEAD. My dull eyes locked on the spot where the floor met the tile wall in front of me.

I was the reason he fell. Even if I was being mind controlled by Anacora, I was the one who told Anacora Gabriel's plan of overthrowing Him. I betrayed him.

After a brief reunion with the rest of the Swans and dinner, I lay awake in bed. I kept falling asleep and waking up over and over. At least I had some soup in my belly. I hadn't had time to think about how starved I was until I had two cans of soup, and Theo ate even more than I had.

It was strange how different this room was compared to the one I'd first stayed in. It had a bed on one side and a bookshelf and a desk on the other. It was almost like... I lived here now.

I gazed at the ceiling, replaying the unbelievable events that had led me here. Todd's murder, Heather and Aaron's rescue, and the raid that made us lose Gabriel.

Gabriel.

I SAT *in a chair in our hut built with mud. Leo, and his brother, Gabriel, stood in front of me. My parents perched nearby, watching closely.*

One of the twins held the flower in their hands. The petals were white, and the bulbs were small compared to the leaves surrounding it. The phralda didn't look like much, but it would decide everything.

I gulped.

One of them gave it to me with a gentle smile. "Here you go."

I reached out, but hesitated to grab it. One set of golden eyes stared at me with glaring impatience. The one who gave me the flower kept smiling, though. That was comforting, and ultimately coaxed me into grabbing the shrub.

I looked down at the plant and gasped. The leaves shot out in droves. I dropped it out of shock.

The man's smile widened. "Looks like you're a healer," he said. "And an amazing one at that."

Me, a healer? But Mom and Dad were fighters.

The other twin looked away with a scowl. He had to be Leo. He always had that serious look on his face.

"Yes!" Dad threw up his arms and ran towards me. He picked me up and hugged me tightly. "I'm so proud of you."

He was?

I wrapped my arms around his neck with a laugh of relief. My mother joined the hug with her gentle touch. I was so happy they were proud of me.

THE HUT SHADED us from the heat of the desert. I sat on my knees. My father perched his arm on the armchair in front of me.

The deep cut on his arm seeped a burning sensation into his skin. I held my palms up to the gash and closed my eyes. When I opened them, the shining wound was gone.

"Remarkable." My father grinned at his arm with incredible pride before switching his bright gaze to me. "You're destined for great things, Caleb."

I glanced away and fidgeted with my fingers. "Mm-hm."

"Come now, he's only fifty-one." Mom stood in front of the door. She had returned from training a couple moments ago. Her long, black hair was tied back into a ponytail. "All he should worry about right now is being a kid."

"I know, I know," my father said. "He just has such amazing talent."

He smiled at me with his glistening blue eyes as his hand patted my head. "Don't ever forget how special you are. No matter what other people tell you."

I smiled and leaned onto the armchair with my father's hand resting on my head. "I won't, Father."

WE STOOD outside our hut in the rocky desert. Father gritted his teeth. His eyes shook with rage. "What do you mean you won't join?"

I held my wrists tighter. "I can't support what the Sanandum does," I said. "Healing angels to fight and kill each other isn't right."

His fists trembled, but he didn't move.

Mom stepped into my view from the hut. Her brows curled with concern. "Is all of that true?" she asked me.

If anyone could understand, then it would be her. "Yes."

She didn't say anything. Neither of them did. Until she appeared in front of me and slapped me onto the ground. "So, that's what you think?" she screamed. "Angels fight for their honor and our Gods. So don't go talking like that!"

My cheek smashed into the jagged ground. My other cheek stung from her slap.

I wanted to object, to tell her that violence only fed the flames, but I kept my mouth shut. No one was ever going to understand.

I SAT ON THE DOCK, *looking down onto the reflection of the full moon in the clear, still water. The forest always managed to clear my head, especially when not a single soul was in sight.*

I couldn't go back into that house. Maybe I could live with Naomi? We had already been discussing it for a while now. My parents were the only ones stopping me before and I couldn't bring myself to listen to them anymore.

"What are you doing out here?"

I looked in the direction of the voice. Gabriel stood on the dirt meeting the dock. At least, I assumed it was Gabriel. With that smile, it had to be.

I looked back at the water. "My parents... I fought with them."

"Really?" He stepped onto the wooden dock and sat down next to me. "What about?"

My gaze shifted toward him. Why did he care so much? And why was he here of all places? But his warmth soon dissuaded me from thinking of any more questions.

"They want me to join the Sanandum, but I can't." My brows burrowed into my nose. "The violence sickens me."

I dipped my toes into the water. Ripples disturbed the lake.

My eyes widened when I realized who I was talking to. "Not that there's anything wrong with it. I just can't stand the sight of blo—"

"Don't worry about it." Gabriel waved his hand. "There's nothing wrong with standing against violence."

My jaw dropped. He was the founder of the Sanandum, but he was okay with me not joining?

He put his hand on my shoulder. "Just make sure that you use your talent to help others."

For some reason, my father's blue eyes appeared in my head in that moment. I choked on a lump in my throat, burying my tears. "I will."

THOSE MEMORIES SANK MY STOMACH. Tears gathered in my eyes, but I wiped them away before they could fall. Crying wouldn't help, but what could I do to help? Was there *anything* I could do?

Gabriel was my mentor, no, my friend, and I made him fall. I closed my eyes and begged as if he was right in front of me.

"Please. Be alive."

CHAPTER

TWENTY-THREE

I opened my room's door and drowsily stepped into the corridor. None of the others were in sight.

I stood there by myself, wondering what the hell we were supposed to do now. We knew where Gabriel had been taken, but at the same time, we didn't. Where was the Subplicium? How would we figure it out? Searching blindly would do us no good.

"Caleb."

I looked up. Theo sprinted towards me with his arms flailing above him.

"*Caleb!*"

The closer he got, the faster he ran. I took a step back, afraid that he'd tackle me to the ground. "Theo, what the fuck are you—"

He braked right in front of me, almost tripping me over.

"Theo! Why are you—"

"We have a lead!"

My heart stuttered in my chest. Before I could get any words out, he turned around and charged in the other direction. "Come on!"

We had a lead? How?

The corners of my lips shot up as I chased after him.

WE SAT at the table centered in the common room. The anxious tension in the room mixed with a strange excitement. We finally had a lead.

"Another one of my informants told me approximately where the Subplicium is," Aaron started. Exactly how many informants did he have?

"Well, where is it?" Ethan asked.

"On the coast of southern Chile."

"*That's* all we have to go on?" Theo's voice was just below a yell. "How are we supposed to go off of that?"

"I know, I'm sorry," Aaron said. "But that's all the information we have."

"What's the plan once we get there?" I asked.

"We'll sneak in. Ethan and I will be in charge of taking out any guards before they spot us," Aaron said.

"And what about me?" Theo asked, looking offended.

"You'll cover our backs while we cover the front," Aaron answered.

Theo nodded without complaint, which was weird. There wasn't time to dwell on it, though.

"You guys might want to bring your swimsuits," Aaron said. It sounded like a bit, but he wasn't smiling. Neither was anyone else.

Heather leaned back. "Don't tell me…"

"Yes." He nodded. "It's underwater."

I blinked. "What? How?"

"The building is blessed so that angels around it can breathe underwater," Aaron explained. "Fortunately, when something gets blessed, it doesn't discriminate against certain angels, so it'll work for us as well."

I had no idea Gods could bless entire buildings, never mind an underwater one. How did the Ravens get access to such a place anyway?

"It's a smart move, to be underwater." Ethan rubbed his fingers on his chin. "But how did they manage to get a blessed building?"

"I'm not sure," Aaron said.

The obvious answer was that Anacora or one of the former Gods gave it to them. Not knowing which God blessed the building was the problem. But it wasn't the problem on my mind.

"Hopefully, we'll find him before it's too late," Aaron finished.

"How are we going to get there?" I asked, ignoring Aaron's comment.

THERE WAS a plane in front of me. I never thought I'd be in a hangar with an actual plane. I'd never seen one in person before now.

It was painted white with the tips of the wings and fin being blue. The plane was only slightly bigger than those in the videos I saw of the Second World War, but it resembled a passenger plane more.

"You guys know how to *fly*?"

"Of course." Theo smirked. "It's easy."

Flying in the clouds when I had my wings and the warm wind blowing gently on my face was something I dearly missed, almost as much as Naomi. But there was no time for reminiscing.

"Let's go," Aaron commanded.

We climbed inside.

The interior had cushioned chairs and tiny round tables covered with blue fabric. The chairs clumped together in groups of four, surrounding the four tables like in a restaurant. Sky blue curtains matched the tablecloths.

"I'll fly first," Nathan said before heading to the cockpit.

I sat down and a humongous weight followed me. Gabriel couldn't be dead. He just couldn't.

I LOOKED OUT THE WINDOW, deep in thought. Bright lights shone in the darkness.

We'd stopped to refuel on the outskirts of Havana, Cuba in another Swan base. I had no idea how the Swans could conceal a runway this close to a city, or how they even had the money to have a plane in the first place, but those weren't the most pressing things on my mind.

Before I fell, Gabriel had supported me when my father didn't. My father wanted me to have fame and glory, like he had. But Gabriel had supported, and even encouraged, my ideal of helping others without expecting anything in return or forcing them to fight.

And after I fell and my memories were stripped from me, his warmth comforted me while I was re-entering into this world.

I didn't appreciate it nearly enough at the time. I didn't appreciate his enthusiastic smile enough, either.

"How are you feeling?" Heather asked from the seat next to me.

"I'm feeling..." I tried to find the perfect word. So many descriptions came to mind, but nothing was quite right. Guilty? Shameful? Reminiscent?

"Horrible." My eyes dropped to the edge of the window. "Yeah, horrible," I repeated.

"Me too. I hope we're not too late."

Heather clasped her hands in her lap and stared at them. The color in her eyes had a gray tone to them. I put my hand on her shoulder. She turned her head towards me.

"He held his own against Leo. We have to have faith in him," I said, masking my own persistent doubts.

Tears welled in her eyes, but a smile peeked onto her lips. She flung her arms around me and squeezed. I hesitantly hugged her back.

The empty void inside me grew as we embraced. I missed my soulmate, now more than ever.

THE PLANE SPED toward the ground. An uneasy feeling filled me as we landed.

We had flown for two straight days. Two days of wondering, hoping, if Gabriel was still alive. Two days of feeling like crap for what I'd done to betray one of my role models. Two days of agony.

Yet, when the plane hit the runway, anger spread throughout my entire body. At Anacora, whom Gabriel tried to overthrow, and Leo, who was planning on killing his own brother.

Nathan sat next to me while Heather flew the plane. That gave me some needed comfort. Theo was across from me while Aaron and Ethan sat in another cluster. As soon as we slowed to a cruising speed, we locked eyes with each other.

We would rescue him. We had to. And if he wasn't there, the Ravens would *pay*.

The plane stopped and everyone stood up. The engines turned off, and Heather emerged from the cockpit.

We departed the plane together—afraid and pissed off.

CHAPTER
TWENTY-FOUR

Mountains topped with snow towered in the distance. Mossy trees surrounded the desolate runway. The sandy beach stretched out in front of us, the cold waves splashing onto my feet.

Everyone was already in their swimsuits. Anticipation bounced around in my head as I thought of countless ways this could've gone.

If Gabriel was here, then there was a possibility that... that he was already gone. Guilt gutted me at that image.

"Let's go in first, Ethan," Aaron said.

Ethan nodded before they jumped in together. Then the others followed. I took in a sharp breath as I shoved my emotions away and dived in.

The saltwater blasted my eyes. Every urge in my body told me to swim back up, but I didn't. My lungs stung as much as my eyes. I needed air. Just one, clear breath. But I swallowed back my impulses and swam lower. Lower.

The pressure of the ocean was insurmountable. I blinked but it barely helped the stinging in my eyes. Slowly, my eyes felt less and less irritated as I adjusted to the saline.

A soft, bright light shone along the seafloor, but it was so far down. It shouldn't have been this deep if we jumped in from the shore.

Heather's eyes landed on me. "You can breathe now."

I swallowed the surprised scream in my throat. We could talk, too?

I breathed in, ignoring my instincts, and it was as if I was breathing air. She was right.

"Thank you," I said.

Instead of answering me, she focused on swimming lower—deeper. So did I. Everything around me became clearer, even the fish swimming around us.

"Quiet, everyone," Ethan whispered. "We have to get the jump on them."

A tense silence swooped in after that. I could breathe and see, but we had no idea how many guards surrounded this place. There wasn't a lot of cover either, other than some coral.

We softly landed onto the sandy floor behind one of the few lumps of coral.

The Subplicium was designed like a courthouse—a black courthouse. People died here. I sensed the death radiating from it. Gabriel *couldn't* be among them.

My heart stopped. In the short time that we'd been here, we'd already been surrounded.

Men and women covered the space around us like a cage. Where had they come from?

"You must think I'm stupid."

No.

Chills crawled down my spine, all because of that voice.

"Or you're the idiots for coming here willingly."

Leo stood on the roof of the slaughterhouse, gazing down on all of us.

"And I know I'm *not* stupid," he said.

Leo. He went after me at the Tenebris, even though Aaron was the one attacking him.

I flinched. He wanted to take away my memories, didn't he? That was the only reason he would've had to switch his attention from Aaron's assault to me. I couldn't let him take them. They were the only key to Naomi, and myself.

Theo walked out of the useless cover of the coral. "Where is he?"

Leo scoffed. "We take in lots of traitors every day. Heretics. Murderers." He scowled. "*Thieves*." His sneer turned into a smug smile. "I'm going to need more information."

By the way Leo was taunting us, Gabriel had to be here.

"You fucking asshole." Theo curled his fists. "I'll kill you."

"Do you know why we didn't evacuate after we knew you were coming?" Leo ignored Theo's threat without a second thought. "Because you're going to serve as an example to all the traitors out there. Defiance will not be tolerated." His eyes narrowed. "I'll kill *you*."

Theo bared his teeth. His hands trembled, but he forced himself to step back.

Theo, Ethan, and Aaron formed a tight circle behind the coral, while Heather, Nathan, and I stood inside it. They spotted us, so it was useless to sneak around now. We had to fight.

I need to focus.

But that was easier said than done. My wrists trembled with anxiety and hate. Two intense emotions crashed inside me, but I had to ignore them both.

The Ravens above us laughed. This attempt was useless. That was their message to us. Maybe it was true.

But then, there was silence. The gritting silence before a fight only exaggerated my fear.

The Ravens rushed in. They viciously pounded on Aaron, Ethan, and Theo. Lights flashed. All they could do was block, and all I could do was watch. I felt each strike. Even though the pain was more manageable than before, it persisted on dragging me down.

The Ravens above us charged toward me. Their hands reached for me. Why did they want to take my memories away so badly?

Asking that wouldn't help me now. I tightened my fists. Even if I had to use my bare hands, I would fight in order to see Naomi again.

Nathan swam up and attacked the Ravens ruthlessly before I could do anything. That caught them off guard, but they piled up on him. Nathan couldn't dodge all their blows.

Blood leaked from his temple from a vicious blow. He passed out.

"Nathan!"

They tossed him away like garbage. A flash of anger pushed my foot up.

But Aaron jumped before I got anywhere, pushing me back down on his way up. He slashed the Ravens with his whip of light. Blood splattered across the crowd.

He pushed higher to engage with more of the enemy, but that left an opening on the ground. Right where Heather was.

She pulled out two sharp, metal knives from her bottoms. Her *bottoms?* She fought off the Ravens skillfully with her blades, but someone slashed across her arms. And everyone else had bruises from blocking the attacks.

I winced, but I shoved the yelps back down my throat. *Pull it together.* Now was my chance. I had to get Nathan back to the safety of the circle while I could.

I jumped up. Ethan yelled something, but I kept pushing through the crowd. My heart thumped as Ravens lunged at me. I swerved and dodged.

Nathan lay in the sand. His face was swollen from strikes.

Grab him and go. Grab him and go.

My hands reached for him. Someone swooped in to snatch my hand, but I braked just in time. I caught a glimpse of the Raven when I did.

Fear widened my eyes as Leo stared back. Everything was in slow motion, even the background noise.

He could take my memories away, and he would stop at *nothing* to do that. I would lose myself. Again.

The air in my lungs tightened before I reached for Nathan. *Grab him.* There was no time for fear.

I fell face-first into the sand and I scrambled onto my feet.

Leo held Nathan back by his arms. His bruised face turned toward me. Naomi's little brother, in enemy hands.

My arm trembled. Anger stirred inside me, but I had too much fear to move.

What should I do?

My arms were yanked behind my back before I thought of something. I struggled against the Ravens holding me, but their grips wouldn't break. I raised my leg to kick them off of me.

My shoulders snapped before I could. A sharp scream bellowed from my mouth. Pain exploded throughout my back. I shoved more screams down my throat as the agony coursed into my lungs and loudened my breath.

They dislocated someone's shoulders? No. They broke them, and they fainted from the pain.

Aaron.

Another burst of pain caught me off guard. They were moving his arms to intensify the pain. And even though he had passed out, I could still feel it.

So, even Aaron was captured?

Leo tossed Nathan to someone.

"You're sensitive." He narrowed his eyes with an evil smirk. "So, I wonder what you'll feel if we break someone's spine."

A stream of air shot out of my nose. I tried to project anger and confidence, but we were royally screwed. Leo never bluffed. I remembered that much.

Leo moved out of the way to reveal my friends forced to the ground. Ravens stood on top of them, holding their arms behind their backs.

Aaron was unconscious, along with the battered Nathan. The ones that had tried to protect me only ended up looking like that.

"There's no escape this time. Sarhiel is the only reason you won at the Tenebris, and now we have him."

Nathan had his face shoved in the sand. It was my turn to protect them.

"Please. Just—"

"You know what I want," Leo said.

My memories. He would spare them if I gave him my memories. Was that really the price I had to pay?

I couldn't give up my only chance to see Naomi again, but I couldn't watch them die either. She wouldn't forgive me for letting her little brother die, and neither would I. I would also miss Theo's loud complaints and Ethan's insight, Heather's calming smile and Aaron's fierce comradery and leadership. And after Leo killed them, the chance of me escaping with my memories was slim at best.

There was no choice. I sighed, closed my eyes and conjured up the last memory of her I'd ever see.

THE STARS TWINKLED in the dark glow of the night sky. Naomi's roof offered the perfect view. Even so, all I could focus on was the

wisps of her hair on my arm, her shoulder leaning against mine, and the soft smile on her face.

"Naomi."

She looked at me with those sparkling-brown eyes. "Yeah?"

I pulled out the flower from my pocket. Glowing particles swam around the golden stem and violet petals.

Her eyes sparkled in awe. I inched it toward her, and she put her hand on her chest. "For me?"

"Yes."

Slowly, she grabbed the flower by the base of the petals. She followed one of the orbs surrounding it with her eyes.

"What are these?"

"It's pollen," I said. "It helps the flower search for its other half. That way, they can have kids."

She laughed. "That's a weird way to describe love." She scooped the flower to her nose and took a long sniff then a relaxing exhale before she turned to the stars.

I followed her gaze to the sky with a warm smile on my face.

She would never forgive me if I let them die, but I had to know.

I opened my eyes. "We came here for Gabriel. Give him back."

Leo stared at me with a rock-hard frown, but somehow, I knew he wouldn't hurt me. He would've already if he wanted to.

His eyes softened a little. "Very well." He looked at one of his men. "Bring out the traitor." The Raven swam inside the Subplicium, far from my view.

"I'll let you see him before I take your memories," he said. "That'll be much more satisfying."

The other Ravens had the exact smile Leo had: a cunning twist of lips filled with hatred and pure *joy*.

A disgusted feeling squirmed in my gut. My wrists cramped as Theo struggled against his captors. They contorted his wrists, but their grins revealed they wanted to do so much more. Why they didn't was beyond me.

Theo surrendered and glanced up. His eyes widened with horror.

My eyes darted over. A woman stood there with devious shadows covering her grinning face. She held something up by its locks.

Gabriel's lifeless *head*.

A devastated noise escaped my throat. I expected tears to puddle my eyes, but nothing came.

Gabriel's brown eyes weren't brown anymore. They were a dull gray. Lifeless. *Dead.*

Blood dripped out from his decapitated head and swirled in the water.

My entire body shook.

Dead. Dead. *DEAD.*

My stomach ripped itself apart. Puke bubbled in the back of my throat, but I couldn't stop looking at him. At his *head*.

We were supposed to save him. He wasn't supposed to die.

"You said you wanted him back." Leo stared me down. "There he is."

Rage burned in my throat as I shook violently against the Ravens holding me back. How could he do this to him? To his own brother?

He gave me a taunting smirk before appearing in front of me and putting his hand on my head. I was going to forget everything. Right after seeing Gabriel's lifeless head, I would forget it all and live as though it never happened.

Naomi.

Blood clouded the water . A horrible ruby red. I stopped and stared at the sight before me.

Aaron had woken up.

His arms stretched out with his shining whips. Tens of Ravens' throats were slit in a single second. How did he get free? And when?

Leo swung around, placing his arm in front of my chest. No one moved. The remaining Ravens stared at Aaron with disbelief and fear.

Then Aaron and the recently freed Swans swam toward the surface. His shoulders throbbed as he did.

A Raven glanced between Leo and my comrades. "Leo, shouldn't we—"

"No. We only need him." Leo looked at me, his eyes still startled from Aaron's surprise attack, but his sinister pride was creeping back. Without warning, he set his palm onto my head again.

Aaron's searing pain faded away as he got farther. Did they just... abandon me? No. They were simply outmatched against Leo. Right?

Naomi. The image of her got further and further as my hope dwindled, and countless questions swarmed my mind. Would they bring me back to the same town? Would they keep me so depressed and isolated that each morning I woke up with a hangover? And would I have another Todd?

But nothing happened.

Leo clenched his teeth as his hand fell back to his side. "Damn it. Those traitors don't know when to give up."

I steeled myself. "What are you talking about?"

No one answered me. Leo gained his composure, but frustration seeped through his voice. "Bring him to a cell."

"But—"

"Just do it." His eyes narrowed. "We *will* find a way."

Ravens dragged me inside the giant, black Subplicium. I barely paid attention to my surroundings as I walked up the steps, made turns into tunnel after tunnel, and was shoved onto a cell floor.

I huddled in the corner of the cell.

They abandoned me. Logic didn't make that statement hurt any less.

The pit in my stomach from seeing Gabriel's lifeless head was relentless, but at least, I still had my memories of Naomi to keep me company. I had to keep it together. *If I can.*

CHAPTER
TWENTY-FIVE

I sat in the desolate cell, replaying what had occurred in my head.

Gabriel was dead, and it was all my fault. His laugh that lightened any heart would never be heard again. His golden eyes would never sparkle again.

I studied the steel bars preventing me from escaping. I sighed and closed my eyes. No one else would die as long as I stayed here.

But what about Naomi? No, maybe... *she's better without me.*

Torchlight seeped through my eyelids, but I didn't bother opening them. My eyes felt so heavy. Everything did.

The light burst. I jumped. I tried forcing my eyes open, but all I managed was a squint. Every corner of my cell was covered in white light.

What was happening? The light shrank into a bright shadow of something. A woman?

It slowly dimmed until the light outlined her complexion. Her blonde hair and ceremonial white dress flowed freely in the water. Her crystal blue eyes offered a friendly warmth.

No way. It was Her. Lady Elisha. But how? She was dead. She'd been dead for years.

She smiled. "Hello, Caleb."

I stuck to the wall like glue. "How are You here?"

"I'm here to help you." Her brows furrowed. "You need to break out of here."

My trembling stopped. Why would the spirit of Lady Elisha want to help me? If I escaped, Leo would keep hunting me down, and my friends would keep getting hurt.

I frowned and turned toward the wall. "That's a stupid reason to come back to life."

"No, it isn't." Those words boiled my blood with rage. "Your friends haven't given up on you."

"Well, they *should*."

"Caleb!" I flinched. "This is an order from your former God. You *must* escape."

My shoulders sank as I remembered. I remembered Gabriel's lifeless head floating in the water. I couldn't let that happen again with anyone else. "No." My arms squeezed into my sides. "No more."

Her fierce stare burned through my back, but it was okay. My friends were safe.

"They're your friends. They're supposed to help you."

"Is that what You think?"

"Yes. Friends are willing to sacrifice for one another. That's what they're supposed to do."

"Exactly. This is what *I'm* supposed to do."

"So, you're willing to let their efforts go to waste?"

"If it means that they'll be safe, then yes."

"Even Sarhiel?"

I looked over my shoulder into Her diamond eyes. *Sarhiel.*

"Maybe." I thought about it a little longer. "He did save my life, though, so..." I paused. "Yes."

She glared at me.

I saw Aaron's betrayal in my dreams. I saw him fight Lady Elisha without holding back, and I saw him kill Her.

"Do *You* want him safe?"

She was talented at hiding Her emotions. Still, I knew She hid something, but I wasn't sure if it was pain or anger or something else entirely.

"I don't know," She admitted.

"Oh."

Her brows burrowed into Her nose, burying whatever emotions She had. "I don't have much time. Your friends are on their way here as we speak."

My eyes widened. They came back for me? Of course, they did. Did they at least heal themselves?

I covered my face with my palms. "Those *idiots*."

"You must not waste their efforts. You must go with them."

I faced her, rage and agony pulling me. "Why? Why am I so important anyway? I just want to forget everything that happened. Why won't You let me?"

"Because you need to save her. Save Naomi."

Naomi. Why was it so surprising to hear her name out loud? She was the reason I went to the Raven strongholds in the first place.

She's better without me.

My brows scrunched. What was I saying to myself? Was *that* what I truly thought?

No. Just earlier today, I was relieved to have my memories still of her with me, although I wasn't exactly sure why they weren't taken away from me. Why did I suddenly start thinking any differently?

I squeezed my hand. "You're right," I said with an airy gasp.

She smiled warmly.

"I'm sorry. I don't know what—"

"Anacora." Her friendly smile was replaced with a determined frown. "Some of His influence is still in you."

"Really? Shit…" Would he be able to possess me again, like when I snapped at Heather?

"Don't worry. It seems He can only suggest you. He doesn't have a complete hold on your mind. And if you stay determined, you should be able to resist it."

"Are You sure?"

She nodded.

Despite that, it was more than slightly unnerving. I barely had a grasp on my own mind, never mind when someone else tampered with it.

"Do you know where Naomi is?" I asked.

"Yes." She nodded with worried eyes. "She's in Heaven, with Anacora."

Anacora. Naomi hadn't fallen, but she was up there with Him. What if He was the reason she called out to me?

"My time is up." Her blue eyes lit up as She smiled one last time. "Good luck, Caleb."

The light illuminating Her spread up Her arms and legs until it completely covered Her body. Then the light tore apart and blew away like embers.

As I watched her fade, a strange sadness stirred inside me, but I had to stay focused. For Naomi's sake.

Quiet footsteps approached from the left. It had to be them. I ran up to the bars and gazed out. They walked—or, more like bounced—toward me carrying a dimly lit torch. Wait, a torch underwater?

"There he is!" Heather pointed.

They approached me. Nathan wasn't with them, but Aaron was. His shoulders ached and the pain crashed into his back. Something was wrong with Theo's ankle, too. I felt his pain burrowing into my sole.

"Why didn't you heal yourselves?" I barked harsher than I meant.

"It helps," Aaron said, barely offering any explanation.

All Theo said was, "Just back up, Caleb." There was no way I would argue with Theo.

I obeyed, and he reached over his shoulder. He pulled a sword out in front of him. Not a sword made of light, but a real, metal sword.

"I'm glad I brought this old thing along."

Why did he bring a real sword? Was this cell protected against divine attacks like the Tenebris was?

He swung at the bars relentlessly before I could question it. The clashing of metal echoed around the hallway. Guards shouted in the distance, but the bars were whittling down.

"Hurry up," Ethan said.

"I'm trying."

The bars suddenly fell toward me. Aaron caught them and pulled them out. Pain reverberated from his shoulders as he threw them away.

Heather waved me over. "Come on."

I nodded and moved out of the cell. The shouting grew closer.

"Let's get out of here," Ethan said.

We ran around the narrow corridors. The wrathful cries of Ravens chased us. After a sharp turn, the entrance appeared. A crowd blocked our escape.

Theo and Ethan pushed in front of us. Ethan's blade of light appeared.

"Stay behind us," Theo demanded.

We rammed into the crowd. The twins clashed with the Ravens, while Aaron counteracted the ones chasing us from behind.

A cacophony of pain screamed around me. It stabbed through Aaron's shoulders, seared in Theo's ankle, and I even felt the wounds of the Ravens. Death already radiated from this place, and we were making it worse. *I* was making this worse.

Heather grabbed my hand. "Stay close to me."

Heather's hand was a sudden comfort among the bloodshed. Maybe I could endure it.

I nodded.

Theo shoved through the last of the crowd. "Go!"

Heather pulled me towards the opening Theo had created. She slipped through. Ravens slammed against me. My hand was yanked out of Heather's grip.

She turned around and stretched out her hand. Her eyes widened in terror. I reached out for her, for the exit, but the Ravens shoved me back inside.

"You're not getting away."

My heart pounded against my heaving lungs, but I couldn't give up. Never again.

"Let me out," I growled.

The one who'd spoken to me smirked before his knuckles bashed my face. I fell against someone behind me.

The metallic taste of blood oozed into my mouth. My nose thumped as my face swelled. Each breath only brought more pain as I was forced to breathe through my bruised mouth. *Not again.*

He laughed at how pathetic I was. But I wouldn't give up so easily. I had Naomi to save.

I lunged and jabbed his chin. He fell to the ground in shock.

Another Raven charged at me. Ethan pushed her away.

"Come on." Ethan took my arm and ran. He slashed his sword at the crowd, but they blocked with their light. They wouldn't let us, no, let *me* leave.

Ethan cursed under his breath and squeezed my arm. "Catch him!" He hurled me above the crowd.

I gasped, flinging through the water like it was air. Heather gawked at me from outside of the black slaughterhouse.

I spread my arms. She jogged a few paces back and caught me before I hit the sand. The impact was strangely soft compared to how fast I'd just flown.

She grinned. "You're okay."

"Yeah. Well, mostly." I pointed to my bloodied nose.

Her smile widened for a moment, like she was about to laugh, but not a single giggle came out. What I sensed behind me only confirmed why.

I looked back. The pain I'd been blocking rushed into me. It was slow at first: Theo's ankle was sore and Aaron's shoulders were searing. *Searing.*

His back snapped. I fell. A thousand daggers thrust through his shoulders. The blades dripped with heat and burned into his skin.

I choked down my screams. Why now of all times?

"Caleb? Caleb, what's wrong?"

Heather's voice and the cries of the Ravens slowly came back to me. Still, the pain wouldn't go away.

"Caleb! You have to get up."

Her voice was more urgent now, but I couldn't move. She threw me over her shoulder as the Ravens charged toward us.

She swam up to the surface. They followed close behind.

Aaron's pain eased the farther we got from him. "Heather..." I didn't see them in the crowd. That meant that they were still down there. "Heather..." My hand dropped. "Go back..."

Salt stung my eyes. I forced them shut as we approached the surface, keeping my mouth closed. Aaron's pain trailed after us and another scream escaped me. The water clogged my nose, but that was nothing compared to the piercing, blazing pain. At least the others were resurfacing.

I heaved when we broke through the surface. Water seared my nostrils before gushing from my nose.

The splashing sounds of people surfacing broke me out of my daze. The Ravens. They swam after me.

Heather scrambled toward the beach.

"What's wrong with you, Caleb?" she yelled. "What happened?"

Aaron was close. Too close to tolerate his excruciating pain.

"Aaron." That was all I could say. I wasn't even sure if she understood me.

We reached the beach. She sprinted up the sand with the Ravens close behind.

"Damn it," she hissed. She tossed me against a mound of dirt. The sand punched my back. I winced.

The Ravens didn't hesitate. One grabbed her wrist. She swung one of her knives and sliced his hand. He backed off, but the others closed in. She stepped back until she was right in front of me.

I couldn't do anything to help her, but she didn't back down. Why was I so useless?

The Ravens looked up. Their eyes followed something in the sky. Heather glanced up, too. I wanted to know what she saw, but even the thought of moving my neck was painful.

Aaron was closer than before. A huge blade of light shone in front of us, blocking the Ravens. Was it Aaron?

"Back off," Ethan barked from above us on top of the hump of sand my back leaned against. It wasn't Aaron after all.

As the Ravens slowly backed away, the pain spread. My ears rang with a familiar shattering noise. Aaron was passing out, and so was I.

Damn it.

TWENTY-SIX

I woke up in bed. The fresh linen was heavenly compared to the hard stone floor of the cell. My room had a squared, cream-colored tile floor.

My breathing sharpened. This wasn't my room at the base.

Buildings stacked close together in a bustling city out of the window next to me. People scuttled and cars sped below me.

As my surroundings cleared, a yelp escaped from me. Aches and venomous stings and searing sensations bombarded me. Faces of people I didn't recognize matched with each injury I felt.

Where the hell am I?

The door swung open. Someone dressed as a nurse beamed at the doorway. "¡Está despierto! (You're awake!)" But her smile soon faded. Even if she didn't hear my scream, the tension in my face alone probably displayed my discomfort.

She walked in and stopped by my bed. "¿Cómo lo sientes? ¿Está bien? (How are you feeling? Are you okay?)"

She was speaking Spanish, and I understood it. How? Maybe I learned it before? But how could I understand it without remembering when I'd learned it? Those questions gave me a headache, and that was the last thing I needed with all the pain nearby.

"¿Dónde estoy? (Where am I?)" I asked, barely recognizing my own voice in a different language.

"Está en un hospital de Búhos en Santiago. Sus camaradas están en algún lugar aquí. (You're in an Owl hospital in Santiago. Your comrades are somewhere in here.)"

Good. They were safe.

The nurse stared at me expectantly. I stared back at her, not knowing what else to do. Did she want something?

"¿Lo sientes mejor? (Are you feeling better?)" she repeated.

Shit. I didn't even answer her question.

"Sí. Me siento mucho mejor ahora. (Yes. I'm feeling much better now.)" I didn't feel Aaron's pain anymore. He must've been healed, or he was far away. Either one seemed possible at this point.

She nodded and headed to the door. "Dejaré que ustedes amigos sepan que estás despierto. (I'll let your friends know you're awake.)," she said as she walked away.

"Thank you."

She turned back to me. "De nada. (You're welcome.)" Then she shut the door behind her.

So, fallen angels had hospitals. That was a strange concept. Then again, Owls were the kind to hide in plain sight.

My face felt better, too. They must've healed it while I was unconscious. Although, a few others close-by had some pain in their faces so it didn't help much.

My gaze wondered for a moment before I stared at the sheets covering me.

I couldn't do anything.

I burrowed my brows into my nose. I couldn't do anything to stop the Ravens from killing Gabriel. It was my fault that he was vulnerable in the first place. I couldn't even fight by their side when everyone helped me escape.

What was I good for anyway? Why had Leo and the Cloud agents gone through all this trouble?

The door swung open. I looked up, and Theo's excited face gazed back at me. He was okay.

He grinned. "Caleb." His arms spread out as he rushed to my bed and jumped onto the mattress to squeeze the life out of me.

An awkward laugh crawled out of me. I couldn't dig my arms out from his grip, so I sat there, frozen.

He jumped back onto his feet. "I knew you were going to be okay."

His brother walked through the door. He wasn't as open about it as Theo, but he was just as excited. The smile on his face proved it.

"I'm glad that you're feeling better, Caleb. All of us were worried when you and Aaron passed out."

I nodded and watched the door expectantly, but no one else came through. Not Heather, or Aaron, or *Nathan*.

"Where are the others?"

"Heather is with Aaron. He hasn't woken up yet," Ethan said. "And Nathan is resting."

"So, they're all right?"

He gave a broad smile and nodded.

I couldn't believe it. Everyone was all right. Everyone except Gabriel.

Gabriel. His name alone was enough to shove the relief away. He was dead because of me—because of my weaknesses.

"Hey? Are you awake?" Theo asked as he theatrically waved his arm in front of me.

I let out a nervous chuckle. "Yeah, I'm awake. I'm just relieved that everyone's okay."

Theo grinned. "Me too." Theo put his hand on my shoulder. "We can take you to them if you'd like."

My eyes lingered on Ethan, who didn't seem to be convinced, before I turned back to Theo. "I'd like that."

I swung my throbbing legs over the bed and stood up. Then we walked out into the hallway together. People dressed in lab coats and white dresses darted across the halls.

I tried my best to hide the pain poking and prodding at me. My father had made sure that my sensitivity wouldn't stop me from performing everyday tasks, no matter how much it hurt. At the time, I despised when he'd made me watch the Pugnare soldiers attack one another, spilling their own comrades' blood, but I understood why he'd done it. He wanted me to be great.

They led me around a corner and toward a dead end. We stopped at the second-to-last door.

"This is Nathan's room," Theo said before opening the door and entering.

My lips spread into a grin as I heard his name. Ethan followed his brother, and I raced after him.

But I froze in the doorway when I saw Nathan lying in a hospital bed. I sensed no pain from him, but I remembered what he'd felt when he got pummeled because of *me*.

I opened my mouth to speak, to tell him how grateful I was and how happy I was that he was okay, but nothing came out. *I did this.*

Nathan noticed me standing there. He smiled when he saw me, but that warm smile soon deteriorated into a frown. His eyes analyzed me with a confused expression.

Theo looked even more confused. "What's wrong, Caleb?"

"I—"

I almost got him killed.

I bolted down the hall before I could stop myself. People whizzed past me. I twisted and turned without thinking about where I was going. I just had to get away from them. The agony hammering me down only reminded me of everything I'd done.

Gabriel's severed head hung in front of my face. His blood swirled in the water and choked my senses.

I put my hand in front of my mouth to stop myself from gagging and kept walking. People stared at me and talked about me with disgusted faces, so I dropped my hand.

Nathan got pummeled because of me. It was my fault.

Shut up. Lady Elisha said friends did that for one another. I would've protected Nathan, too, if I had to.

But you didn't.

Nathan locked his eyes onto me, but his body was gone. His head was decapitated just like Gabriel's. Just like Gabriel. Just like Gabriel.

I bumped into someone. My eyes didn't wander from the floor. After everything that had happened, I thought that the mess in my head was fake, that I'd left it behind at that awful place, but maybe it was inside me all along. Maybe I was crazy after all.

"Sorry," I whispered before walking around them.

"Caleb?"

I stopped because of that familiar voice. I turned around and looked at Heather's dark eyes. She examined me with a concerned expression. "What happened? Are you all right?"

I didn't know what to say.

"Um..." What if I got her killed, too? "I thought you were with Aaron." *You will.*

She nodded. "I was. I just got off the elevator."

"The elevator?" I repeated, still dazed from the pictures plaguing my head.

She stepped closer. "Caleb. Tell me what happened."

I couldn't. Even if I did, she wouldn't understand. None of them would. They were so strong and fearless. They were willing to put their lives on the line for me.

Everything is my fault.

"Nothing. I was on my way to see you and Aaron. I didn't expect to see you here, is all."

"*Caleb.*" She sounded angry now. She looked angry, too, with her brows digging into her nose.

I couldn't tell her. "I—"

"Caleb."

My lips pressed together. She wouldn't let this go. Not until I told her the truth.

"I saw Nathan. And I—" *Just say it.* "I ran away."

One side of her mouth rose into a sneer. "Why?"

"Because everything bad that's happened, it's all my fault. Gabriel getting killed, Aaron breaking his shoulders..." My surroundings faded as I sank deeper into the truth of those words. "Everything."

"Caleb." She placed her hand on my shoulder.

Her face refocused into view. She didn't stare at me with pity or disgust. In fact, she was smiling.

"Before we even met you, we've always put our lives on the line for what we believed in. You know what that means, right?"

No, it couldn't be. Why would she, or any of them, think that after everything I put them through?

"We believe in you."

But those words sounded so genuine. They couldn't be fake. Not with that peaceful expression on her face.

Before I could think, the corners of my lips crept up into a smile. "Thank you."

Her hand dropped to her side before her head jerked behind her. "Come on. You can show me the way there."

I cringed. "I actually don't remember where it is."

She giggled and started walking. I followed. "Don't worry. I visited his room earlier."

"That's a relief."

We walked back in silence, but it wasn't awkward at all. It was nice. The bloody images that kept haunting me didn't come back. But still, the closer we got to Nathan's room, the more anxiety I felt. An apology or a thank you wouldn't be enough. I didn't know what to say to make it up to him. He'd done so much for me, and I didn't do anything to deserve it.

We turned into the hall of his room before I could think of an answer. Ethan stood guard at the door.

He looked at me with that same worried expression he'd given me earlier. When we stopped close to him, his eyes shifted to Heather. "How's Aaron doing? Did he wake up?"

"Yes. He woke up a couple minutes ago. And I heard Caleb woke up, so I came down to see him and ran into him along the way."

"Did he not want to come down?"

"No. He's a little groggy right now."

Ethan nodded and slowly turned his attention to me. Nothing on his face gave away exactly what he was about to do or say, but I knew something was coming.

"I sent Theo down to the cafeteria," he said. "He's been complaining about how hungry he is. It was getting annoying."

My brows scrunched in confusion.

His head tilted to the door. "You can talk to him in private."

He knew. Ethan knew I didn't want to talk about it with him. He knew the only person I wanted to talk with was Nathan.

"Thanks."

He smiled and walked away with Heather beside him back the way we came, and I watched them until they were out of sight.

It was time to face Nathan alone. I took in a deep, steady breath and grabbed the door handle.

I'm going to get him killed someday.

I pushed the door open.

Nathan rested in the same hospital bed. He looked at me with gentle eyes. They almost looked sad. Melancholic, perhaps.

"Hi," he said.

"Hi."

Our gazes locked onto each other. I had no idea what to say, and neither did he. Naomi's face flashed in my head before I spoke.

"I'm sorry."

"Why?" he asked.

I saw the pictures in my mind as I walked into his room and the door closed behind me. "I couldn't help you. All I could do was wait until you got hurt."

His gaze grew distant, a sad smile growing on his lips. "She said you hated fighting. That you didn't want any part in it." His eyes focused on me. "I guess that's changed."

He was right. That was how I used to think. But when negotiation was impossible, and lives were on the line—lives that I deeply cared about—fighting was the only solution. And it was the one thing I couldn't do.

I stepped closer to his bed and analyzed a tiny scar on his cheek. Curiosity grew inside me.

"How did it feel when you found out you were balanced?" I asked.

His eyes wandered until he stared at the sheets covering him. "It surprised me. I thought I was destined to be a healer. So did my parents." He smiled. "So did Naomi."

He shook his head as his grin grew. "But they were so proud of me. And it made me so happy." His nostalgic smile sank into a thoughtful frown.

My parents were proud of me, too, in a way. They wanted me to have glory and fame. I just wanted to help people.

"I wish I was like you." I sat down near the foot of his bed. "Maybe if I could use the light to fight, I could've saved him."

"Gabriel was the strongest one of us. There was nothing any of us could've done."

I clenched my fists, my arms rigid. Maybe he was right, but still.

"I'm glad you're okay," he said.

I turned my head to him. There wasn't even a drop of worry in his eyes. Though, I couldn't help but wonder if he was only hiding his worry.

The smile on my face masked the grief I buried deeper. "I'm glad that you're okay, too."

TWENTY-SEVEN

Nathan ogled me in his hospital bed. "Lady Elisha showed up to talk to you?"

"Yes." I laughed at his startled face. I'd told him the whole story while sitting on the edge of his mattress—of Her appearing in front of me and telling me where Naomi was. "I'm surprised that I didn't freak out more than I did."

"And She told you that Naomi was in Heaven?"

I nodded with the same goofy smile Nathan had.

He looked away, caught in the wonder of it all. "Wow." His smile slowly faded. "But how are we going to get there? The only way to Heaven is flying there, and..."

I frowned. He was right. I was so excited that I finally knew where she was that getting there had completely slipped my mind.

The door opened. Ethan stood there with a tray of food in his hand.

"I figured you might be hungry." He walked in, and the rest of the group trailed behind.

I took the tray from his hands, trying to hide the disappointment on my face. "Thanks."

"They have showers, too," Theo said. Now that he mentioned it, his hair looked a little wet. "No offense, but you need one."

Heather elbowed him with a scowl. "Ow," he said as he rubbed his arm.

I forced a smile. "Thanks a lot, both of you."

Aaron was there, too. His lips quirked up. "Hi Caleb."

There was no pain in his back anymore, so his shoulders were healed after all. "Hi," I responded.

Someone knocked on the door. "¿Puedo entrar, por favor? (May I come in, please?)" Maybe it was a nurse.

"Sí," Nathan answered.

So Nathan understood Spanish, too. Did angels automatically understand all languages, or did he learn Spanish as well?

I sat up from Nathan's bed. My sore butt told me I'd been there for longer than I thought. I examined my tray of mashed potatoes and chili and dug in. It was a little bland, but my empty stomach was still grateful.

"Quería hacerles saber que todos ustedes son libres de irse. (I wanted to let you know that you're all free to go.)"

"Yes." Theo's arms shot up. "I've been waiting for them to say that."

The nurse chuckled under her breath. My theory of angels understanding all languages seemed more plausible now.

Nathan sat against his pillow. "Maybe you can show me where the showers are, too," he told Theo.

Theo turned to Nathan and stuttered over his words. "Uh, y-yeah. Of course."

THE SILKY CLEAN hospital clothes were heavenly compared to my grime-filled garments. Then again, even my own clothes were clean now. I held them in my hand. And for once in a long time, I smelled and felt fresh.

I stood against the wall in the waiting room. Nathan and I had taken quick showers and then came here. Everyone else was in the bathroom doing who-knows-what, and Nathan sat in a chair far from me, so it felt like I was alone.

How would we get to Heaven? Maybe Aaron knew someone? He seemed to have endless connections.

"Hey, Caleb." Heather smiled at me. Everyone else trailed behind her.

"Hi, Heather."

I shifted my attention to Aaron. This was my chance to ask him. I just had to start. He glanced at me with an inquisitive expression.

Just start.

"What are we standing around here for?" Theo demanded. "Let's get moving."

Theo marched toward the doors. Everyone followed before I could say anything. Even Aaron.

I sighed and reluctantly walked out of the door, relieved to leave the nagging torment of the injured behind.

THE PLANE WAS a few feet away from me on the runway. Everyone else was already jumping inside.

Aaron almost hopped in when I snatched his wrist. Ethan, the only one behind us, raised an eyebrow.

"Can I talk to you for a minute?"

Aaron's emerald eyes had a sad sheen. "Sure."

Ethan froze for a moment then went around us to get on the plane. I heard him say something to the others about leaving us alone. Perfect.

I dropped my arm, and he took a step closer. "What do you want to talk about?"

"I wanted to thank you. Officially. For saving my life."

He smiled warmly. "It's no trouble. You're worth helping."

His compliment caught me off guard. I smiled for one, simple moment.

"Is that all you wanted to say?" he asked.

"Actually, I wanted to ask you something."

"What is it?"

"What's the plan now?"

Aaron looked away. "If we're being honest, I have no idea. We just lost Gabriel, and I don't know where the third big Raven stronghold is." His eyes pierced through me. "Why?"

Was it even worth asking him? For fallen angels, going to Heaven was nearly impossible. We needed an angel to take us there, and what angel would agree to that? But Naomi's life was far more important than worrying about how crazy this favor would sound.

"Do you know a way to get into Heaven?"

His brows curled. "Why would you need to do that?"

I held back for a moment. Why did I hesitate anyway? He already knew about Naomi, so there was no point in hiding it.

"Naomi's up there, and I want to make sure she's safe."

He stared at me with a perfectly neutral expression. I expected shock or more confusion, but instead there was silence. Until he grinned.

"I think I know a way in."

My eyes widened. "Really? But how?" I asked. "And why do you want to help me?"

"That last question is really stupid," he said. "Get on the plane and I'll tell you how, along with the others." He ducked into the plane, leaving me stunned.

He was willing to help me just like that? Why?

It didn't matter. If he knew a way in, then I would get to see her again. I had to save Naomi from whatever she was calling me for.

TWENTY-EIGHT

WE SAT ON THE CUSHIONED CHAIRS OF THE PLANE. AARON stood up to explain the plan to everyone while Heather stood beside him.

"The new plan is to gather the prisoners we set free and invade Heaven," he said.

I analyzed his face for a smile or a laugh, but he was serious. It was one thing to rescuc Naomi, but overthrowing Heaven? The eight hundred or so prisoners wouldn't be nearly enough to counteract Heaven's entire army.

"*What?*" Nathan gawked.

"How would we even get in?" Ethan asked.

"And we don't have nearly enough power for an invasion," I added. We didn't need to invade anyway. Not now, at least.

"And why do we need to invade Heaven?" Theo added.

"Because," Heather spoke, her voice barely a murmur. Why was she answering and not Aaron? Wasn't this a plan he'd just come up with? She swayed nervously on her feet and peeked at me. "Because that's where Caleb is meant to be."

What was that supposed to mean?

"Uh, duh?" Theo said. "All of us are *meant* to be up there, but we fell. Screw that place. Let's go after Leo and make him pay."

All the color drained from her face. There was something else she was hiding. Something I needed to know.

Ethan leaned in. "What do you *mean?*" he asked for me.

The silence stiffened. She turned to him with a trembling frown, making sure to avoid my gaze.

"He's the one. From the legend." A deep sigh rattled her shoulders. "The Great Healer."

Theo jumped to his feet. "What? How is that possible? Didn't he get killed by demons?"

"Yeah," Ethan barked. "And why didn't we know this sooner?"

Theo screamed more words at them with his brother, but their meaning escaped me.

The Great Healer. At the back of my mind, on the edge of my regained memories, I remembered His identity. Or... My identity. If this wasn't a joke. I faintly remembered the legend of the First Ones: the first incarnation of the God currently ruling and His brother, the Great Healer. One was the best fighter in the universe. Of course, the Great Healer was the greatest healer of all time. But the Great Healer was lost forever after the final battle against the demons.

It was inconceivable that any one of us was Him, never mind me. After all, this whole time, all I could do was stand back and heal. I couldn't be a God. The most I'd done was break a wall, which wasn't nearly as impressive as what the rest of them had done constantly.

Had Aaron planned to go to Heaven all along? Was *that* why he was so willing to help me?

Nathan stared at me from across the aisle. A pitiful sadness stirred in his eyes. My jaw tightened. I hated the pity everyone berated me with.

I shot up and shoved Ethan out of the way to grab Aaron's shoulder. "Why?" My hand trembled. "*Why* didn't you tell me?"

He frowned. "I was afraid it would be too much for you. You were already stressed out when we told you that you were an angel."

"So, when were you gonna tell me? Were you *ever* going to tell me?"

His eyes softened. "I'm sorry."

That was all he had to say? He hid my own identity from me, and all he had to say was *sorry?*

My grip crushed his shoulder. Aaron tried to be stoic, but a wounded grunt slipped out as his cramping grew. This odd strength flowing through me felt familiar somehow, like when I smashed through the Tenebris' wall.

Heather touched my wrist. "Stop. He was just doing what he thought was best."

I smacked her hand away. "And how long have you known?" My finger aimed at her chest. "*You* were the first one who assured me there were no secrets. That I finally knew the truth about me. And now, you do this?"

She looked at me with steady eyes. "I've known for a while. Since before we rescued you."

My eyes widened. She knew that far back and never told me? Why?

I turned around. "Did any of you know?"

The rest of them shook their heads. So, they kept it from everyone else, too. What reason could they possibly have to keep something so huge a secret?

I bared my teeth at Aaron. "Why didn't you tell me? You knew how lost I was, so why?"

He said nothing. He just stared at me with that same pitying look. Before I could think, I flung my fist toward his face. Theo appeared in front of me to catch my knuckles.

I swiped my fist out of his grip. Before I could maneuver around him, he blocked me from getting to Aaron.

"Get out of my way."

"It's not worth it," he muttered.

He was wrong. Aaron had this coming.

I looked into Theo's eyes to tell him off, but his eyes reflected a gentle understanding that Heather and Aaron failed to give.

I scanned the group around me. The rest of them had that same look in their eyes. It wasn't just pity that they showed for me. They showed empathy.

Theo was right. What was I thinking? Punching Aaron in the face wouldn't solve anything, no matter how much I wanted to hit something.

What a strange thought. I'd never wanted to hit something, or someone. At least, not from what I could remember.

WATER SPLASHED over my hands as I washed them in the bathroom sink, but it didn't feel like I was moving at all. Maybe I'd been stagnant this entire time.

I turned off the water, wiped my hands, and slid open the door. Aaron stood there. Without acknowledging his presence, I headed back to my seat.

"Caleb, wait."

I stopped. "*What?*"

The others stared at us, clearly expecting a scandal.

"I didn't tell You the whole truth."

I swung back around. "Really? Because I would *never* expect that from you."

He looked at my angry face with shame. "Please. Just let me tell You the rest."

My scowl deepened. I wanted to fight him so badly, but I remembered Theo's words and held myself back.

"Fine." He couldn't say anything worse anyway.

Aaron nodded gratefully and motioned to the seats. I sat down next to Nathan, and Aaron sat across from us by himself.

The twins across the aisle leaned in.

Aaron slowly forced out a deep exhale. "Okay." He nodded to himself before starting. "This all started before I fell. Lady Elisha and I were—" His eyes fluttered around the cabin. "In love."

I sat back, stunned.

WE LOOKED out from Her bedroom balcony. The fields of grass and trees spread across our view. The city towered in the distance.

I breathed in the fresh air. "It looks so beautiful."

"Yes." She nodded with a smile. "It looks even better at night with the stars."

I turned my gaze to Her. Her crystal blue eyes mirrored the sky above.

Her eyes focused on me. "What is it?"

"I can't wait to wake up to this view every morning. And You." I waved to the bed in the middle of Her room, the only thing there besides Her wardrobe and mirror. "You'll be right next to me." A chuckle slipped from me. "I still can't believe it."

"What's so hard to believe?"

"I never thought You'd notice a random angel like me."

Her brows creased. "But you're not random."

I laughed a little. I should've known She'd have a comeback for that.

I wrapped my arm around Her waist and pulled Her in close. She seemed so calm and tranquil, like always. Her cherry pink lips were tantalizingly close, but I—

She kissed me.

Her plump lips softly pressed into mine. My tired eyes relaxed into slits. I breathed in Her familiar lavender scent.

This was... I closed my eyes completely, taking in Her embrace. This was bliss.

I SPRINTED *across the castle ground and spotted Gabriel strolling around. He looked at me strangely, but I hurried past him. There was no time.*

"Are you looking for Her?"

I stopped and turned around. "Yes. Do you know where She is?"

Gabriel grinned. "Last I checked, She was in the courtyard."

I sped off without saying goodbye. I had to hear Her explanation myself.

"Good luck," he yelled behind me.

I flipped around the corner and ran into the courtyard. Lush grass blanketed the ground. Trees were planted at every corner.

She was there. Sitting by one of the trees. A baby played in the grass beside Her with its tiny wings spread out.

I ran to Her. "Elisha!"

She looked up and smiled. "Sarhiel." She jumped to Her feet and spread Her arms out for an embrace.

I stopped out of Her range. "Is this where You've been all day? We were supposed to meet up in the city. I've been worried sick."

Her smile sank. "That was today?"

I froze. It took a moment for those words to sink in. "Yes."

Her arms dropped, and She took a step closer. "I'm sorry, Sarhiel. I forgot."

I pointed at her, warily. "You forgot something?"

She giggled, but I didn't find this funny. She never forgot things. "Yes. It isn't like Me. I promise this will be the only time."

It was truly strange hearing that She forgot something. But as long as She was okay, it didn't matter too much. "Fine." The edges of my lips rose. "I can't stay mad at You anyway."

She nodded and sat back down, patting the spot next to Her. I sat down and watched the unfamiliar baby walk in front of me.

"Whose baby is this?"

"I don't know. I found him on Earth's oceans."

My eyes widened. "What? Why was he down there?" I'd never heard of angel babies riding the waves on Earth. The thought alone seemed ridiculous.

"I wish I knew."

She picked him up when he was in front of Her, and his wings retracted. Then She sat him in Her lap. The baby seemed content there, and adorable.

"But there's something I need to tell you about him," She said.

"What? Is he an orphan?" That much was obvious.

"Yes." She turned to me with compressed brows. "And He's also My brother."

I stumbled back. "WHAT?"

Everyone on the plane stared at him with that same intense look, including me. I couldn't believe what I was hearing.

"At first, I was happy for Her. Surprised, but happy. She wanted to keep it a secret. I'd asked Her why, but all She said was that She didn't want to startle the angels. I thought Her reasoning was strange, but, who was I to disagree? She gave You to a pair of Her guards that acted as Your parents, but She spent a lot of time with You. That's when..." He cringed as his shoulders tensed. "I started getting jealous. I felt like She was shutting me out, for good."

He leaned back into his seat. "And what happened at the tipping point, You already know."

Silence.

So *that* was what triggered him to steal the sword. The Galactica belonged to the Great Healer, and he was jealous of me. Then he killed Her with it out of spite.

"But if I was a baby, then why do I remember Lady Elisha being at my Second Blessing?" I asked skeptically.

"It didn't happen immediately," he said. "It took several hundred years for me to break." He looked away. "I've regretted breaking so easily ever since."

Was he telling the truth? Why didn't I remember spending time with Her like Aaron said I had? I didn't even remember Her death yet, unless I counted seeing Aaron kill Her. Just when I thought I knew myself again, there was a gaping hole in my memories, desperate to be filled.

"I had no idea Gods could have soulmates." Ethan squinted his eyes in thought. "How is that possible?"

"I don't know," Aaron said.

Nathan sank into the chair next to me. "That's insane."

"Totally," Theo agreed.

I buried my head into my palms. "You did it because you were jealous of me?"

He hesitated. "Yes."

I closed my eyes shut. Aaron killed someone out of petty jealousy? His condition was so much worse than any of us could've imagined.

CHAPTER
TWENTY-NINE

I sat on the plane, still stewing in what had been revealed. I was the Great Healer, a God: a God that couldn't even save Gabriel.

Heather flew the plane while Aaron sat in front of me, explaining the plan to get into Heaven in more detail. Heather had been flying it for a while now. Was she avoiding me?

Nathan sat next to me, which was comforting. Theo sat next to Aaron, with his brother sitting alone in the other cluster of chairs.

"We're going to gather all the prisoners we freed from the Tenebris. I've been able to relatively keep track of them," Aaron said.

"By using the radio at the base?" Ethan asked.

"By using the telegraph."

I didn't even know we had those, but it made sense. There were Swan bases all around the world, and they had to stay in contact somehow.

"Then we're going to use Paul to trick an angel to bring us into Heaven," Aaron finished.

"He can do that?" Theo gawked.

He put his palm in front of him. "Only for a couple minutes. Bending someone's perception is much harder than simply communicating through thoughts."

"But where are we going to find an angel?" I asked. Angels that hadn't fallen rarely, if ever, visited Earth.

He sucked his lips. "I know one."

"Really?"

He nodded slowly, like he was stalling for time. Nathan and I exchanged worried glances before switching back to Aaron.

"Well, who is it?" I muttered snarkly.

Aaron closed his eyes and bowed his head with a cringe-filled frown. "It's Leo."

Nathan leaned back in his chair and gazed at the ceiling in complete disbelief. Ethan placed his hand onto his mouth. I rubbed my wrist into my forehead, hoping that massaging it would take back the words he spoke.

Of all people, why did it have to be Leo? Leo was the one who'd killed Gabriel. Leo was the one who hunted us, who hunted me.

"How did that piece of shit get redeemed? He *killed* Gabriel!" Theo snapped.

Aaron shook his head. "All I know is that Anacora redeemed him."

Theo jerked his head away with a growl.

Ethan's stare fixated on empty space. "He's getting more corrupt by the day."

"Yeah," Nathan agreed with a nod.

I put my hands in my lap and rubbed my thumbs against my palms. All of the hints—Lady Elisha urging me to save Naomi, Anacora redeeming a murderer, and this sinking pit in my gut—all of it pointed to something awful.

"We have to stop Him," Nathan said. I couldn't tell if he said that to himself, to me, or to everyone. But did it even matter?

Theo gently pushed his elbow into Nathan's shoulder. "Hell, yeah, we do." He smirked, which made Nathan look away with a red tint on his cheeks.

My irises contracted when recognition struck. Was that what the strangeness between them was?

"Then, with the prisoners, we'll be able to stop Anacora for good." Aaron looked at me with knowing eyes and nodded. Even if Nathan had a crush, it wasn't my biggest concern right now.

This was Aaron's plan all along: to get me back into Heaven so that I could take Anacora's place. I didn't like the way his plan and my identity were revealed, but as long as I got to save Naomi, this plan didn't bother me. Or, at the very least, I could tolerate it.

What came after our insurrection worried me. Leading the entirety of Heaven didn't sound easy, but I couldn't let a case of the zorros stop me from saving Naomi. Not after everything that I'd done so far.

I nodded back.

"So, where are they?" Ethan asked.

"All over," Aaron said. "But as long as they use the Owl tunnels, they should be able to make it back to our base."

Theo grunted. "If we didn't have a telegraph at the base, gathering them would be a pain in the ass."

"So, we're going back to base then?" I confirmed.

Aaron nodded.

Going back and doing more waiting sounded tedious, but not nearly as tedious as flying all over the world would be. Naomi was so close, and yet, so far away.

I squeezed my fists in anticipation.

CHAPTER

THIRTY

"Pudicitiam."

The giant steel wall in front of me slid open as I lowered my hand. I walked inside the common room, my stoicism not reflecting what I felt inside.

Aaron and Heather sat at the table as Nathan hunched over them. "Why didn't you tell Him before?" Nathan questioned.

"I didn't want to overwhelm Him," Aaron said. "I wanted to help gather His memories and have Him choose whether He even wanted to return to Heaven."

"Why wouldn't He—"

Heather noticed me first. "Guys..." Then Aaron and Nathan saw me, too.

I stopped in front of the table. Nathan watched me with that pitiful, sad look on his face. He opened his mouth, as if he was about to say something, but didn't. All Nathan did was pat my back, then walk out of the room, leaving me alone with them.

Aaron analyzed me with careful eyes.

"Was that really why you didn't tell me? You were just waiting until I remembered that I was a fucking *God*?"

He sighed, frowning. "Yes."

It didn't look like he was lying, but I wasn't sure if I could trust him at all anymore.

I turned to Heather. "And why didn't you tell me?"

"Because Aaron asked me to." She grimaced. "I'm sorry. It was wrong."

They kept me in the dark so that I could discover my identity on my own. How fucking demented was that? All this time, I thought that I wasn't strong enough, and they knew all along that I was more than an angel.

I swiped my gaze away from them to contain my anger. That was when I noticed wisps of lights flowing off my hand. I unclenched my fist, rotating my hand and watching the light flow until it faded away.

Heather gawked at me, her mouth dropping to the floor in amazement. Aaron narrowed his eyes.

Even though I was angry at them, there were so many things I had to know. I had to let my curiosity guide me.

"So, if I'm a God, can I use the energy to fight?"

"No," Aaron answered. "Same thing goes for Anacora. He can't use His energy to heal others, but He can take a lot more punishment than an angel can, just like You."

"So, I'm technically stronger than an angel?"

"Yes."

I paused for a moment to think. "If I can't use the energy to fight, then why does the legend say that I have a sword?"

Heather and Aaron looked at each other.

"The Galactica, right?" I pressed.

"We think that the First God tried to make a way for You to fight," Heather answered. "That's why He made You that sword."

I glanced around the room at all the weapons on the walls. The guns made me nauseated, as did the bows, but the swords... I didn't feel sick at all when I looked at them. How did I not notice that before?

"Do You want a sword?" Aaron asked as I admired them. "They aren't as powerful as the Galactica, but—"

"Yes."

They leaned back in surprise. I was slightly surprised myself. I didn't think I'd ever want a weapon near me again, but maybe swords were more comforting because I owned one once, even if I didn't remember it? This was all so confusing.

Heather eventually stood up. "I'll help You pick one out." She walked over to the wall stacked with swords while I followed. They had a large collection, with both western and eastern styles. One stood out to me. A thinner, curved sword with a black sheath decorated with crimson swirls. The handle was wrapped with black hide, which gave it a simpler look.

"I'll try that one," I said, pointing to it.

Heather reached on the tips of her toes and grabbed it off one of the stands bolted to the wall. She handed it to me. I thought the sword would feel foreign in my hands, but the weight and the textures all felt so familiar.

I unsheathed the blade. A wave ran along the edge of the shining steel. The inside of the sheath had been oiled, but why, I didn't know. Still, somehow, this felt right.

Aaron stood up. "Do You know how to use it?"

"I'm not sure," I said, admiring it.

"Then let's find out." Heather revealed her blades and slashed at me. I parried her attack, tossing the sheath onto the ground. She slammed her knives down towards me. I blocked. She dived down and lunged. I spun around her and waved the sword to her back, stopping it inches from her shoulders.

I let out a breath, realizing what I had just done. Did I really win a fight?

Aaron stared at me. "Well, then..."

I dropped the sword to my side and Heather turned around. "Impressive swordsmanship," she complemented with a smile.

I won, but I didn't even know how I did. Maybe it was instinctual. But then, why was my healing blocked until I got my memories? Wasn't healing instinctual as well? None of this crap made sense, but for once, I could fight.

THIRTY-ONE

The common room was hauntingly quiet. Everyone had long been asleep in their rooms. I cut and slashed invisible targets with the sword, spinning my feet along, practicing movements I didn't know I knew. Maybe I was making them up. But it felt like I'd done them before, in a dream.

No, it wasn't in a dream. My victory against Heather proved that.

I stopped swinging, lowering the handle to my pelvis.

That victory was earlier today when the sun was still up. It would take a couple more days until all the other Swans showed up. *What if she doesn't last that long?*

My left hand let go of the sword's handle as the sword dangled at my side.

She was always at the edge of my mind. Naomi's racing fear mixed with my own desperation. Saving her was my mission. I was a God, and that didn't do anything to help.

My heart thrashed in my chest as a consuming rage boiled my blood.

My hand slapped the handle. I swung the blade, imagining

everything that she could've been going through as I waited. But it didn't matter what I imagined. She'd called out for me, and that was all the confirmation I needed that something horrible was happening to her.

The blade zipped through the air.

I couldn't do anything for her right now. *She's probably dead by now.*

A loud cry escaped me as the steel hit the ground. The tip of the blade dug into the metal floor.

No. She wasn't dead yet. I would've known if she was. That thought must've been Anacora's suggestion like Lady Elisha warned me about. That didn't make thinking about her death any easier.

I sighed. No amount of anger would change how much waiting I had ahead of me.

My feet spread apart to pull the sword out of the ground before drops of light swirled around my arms. I let go of the handle and admired the light. It swam around me with a mind of its own. I wasn't trying to use the energy, so why had it appeared now? Maybe it was caused by emotion?

Wind roared behind me, slapping my back with warmth. But there was no wind down here, never mind wind that warm. Goosebumps rattled my skin. A feeling of ecstasy swirled around me. There was only one place I remembered the wind being so warm, but it couldn't be.

I turned around.

Light raced around an opening to that all-too-familiar lake. The starlight reflected perfectly in the water. Pine, oak, maple, sycamore, weeping willows, and many other kinds of trees surrounded it.

Heaven. Heaven was right in front of me.

I picked the sword up as I lifted my foot.

"Caleb!"

I spun around. Nathan stood by the entrance to the room, gawking at the sight before him. "What is that?"

I took a tiny step closer to the portal—a feeble attempt to hide it. His mouth dropped open as the realization struck him. "Is that Heaven?"

I didn't answer, but I didn't need to.

He grinned. "Guys! Caleb opened a portal to Heaven," he shouted to wake the others up before speeding toward me. "This is amazing! We don't even need to use Leo. We could go right—"

"*Stop.*"

Nathan froze at the harshness of my voice.

"What?" he asked. "What is it?"

I narrowed my eyes. "I can't."

"Of course, You can," he answered with a nervous smile. "I know it might be hard to keep it open, but I know what You can do. Even if it's just the seven of us that can—"

"No." His shoulders stiffened. "I can't let you come with me. You and everyone else have been fighting my battles for far too long."

He stared at me for a moment—a moment that seemed to last forever. He grabbed his wrists, a habit he undoubtedly got from his sister. "*Your* battle?"

The light flashed. "I am the Great Healer, aren't I?"

His bottom lip quivered. "But that's my sister up there."

My frown deepened. "I know." But taking down Anacora was my responsibility, not his or anyone else's.

I stepped through the portal and onto the grassy plains. The light shining from the base eventually faded into nothing. The portal closed behind me, leaving him and the others behind.

Something grabbed my ankle. I looked over my shoulder with a groan. "Are you fucking kidding me?"

Nathan gripped onto my ankle. Aaron was right behind him, holding onto a tiny string of his light wrapped around Nathan's foot. All the others followed like a chain, every single one wearing their pajamas. They heaved from exhaustion.

I snatched my foot out from Nathan's grip. "What the hell are all of you doing here?"

They stood up.

"Since when are You so bossy?" Theo asked before smiling. "I like it."

Ethan rolled his eyes before offering an explanation. "Invading Heaven alone is dangerous, even for a God."

"Bull*shit*." A God was much stronger than an angel. Everyone knew that much. Invading Heaven would be much easier for someone like me than a bunch of angels.

"Because we want to support You." Heather stepped closer to me. "Even if you think this is just on Your shoulders, we're Your comrades. We *need* to support each other."

Gabriel's severed head flashed in my mind. "But—"

"Remember when I said that anyone who stops You from pursuing your goal is an asshole?" Aaron said. He never knew that Gabriel said that to me before he did, but I didn't dare tell him now. "Now, *You* have the choice. To let us help You or to make us suffer knowing every possible thing that could go wrong without our aid."

Aaron's shining green eyes burrowed deep into my own.

If he'd forced me to stay cooped up in that room, waiting for answers for an eternity as they fought the Ravens without me, I would never know where Naomi was. I wouldn't even be here. I could've portaled them back if I tried hard enough, back to where they were safe. But if I did that, I'd be an asshole for life.

"Okay." I nodded. "Let's do this."

THIRTY-TWO

We stepped onto the grass. The leaves and the wood of the trees camouflaged us as we approached the city.

"What's the plan here?" Ethan asked. "We're severely outnumbered by ourselves."

Aaron opened his mouth in the corner of my eye. "Just leave Anacora to me," I said before he could get a single word out.

Aaron's gaze shifted to me. I tried my best to ignore his judgment, whatever it was.

I knew that if I fought Him, then I would find and save Naomi. That was the only reason I needed.

The hair on my arm spiked. Something was coming.

"Look out!" I zipped behind us, unsheathing the sword. Leo charged toward me with unbelievable speed. I readied myself to deflect him before someone shoved me out of the way. Light sparked around their green eyes. Aaron.

I hit the ground and jumped back onto my feet. Aaron was standing, but I didn't have to look at his bruised arms to know his pain. He had slid back from the impact Leo dealt him. His forearms were searing, but I'd dealt with worse before.

"So, it's true then." Theo's wide, trembling eyes stared at Leo. "He's been redeemed."

"Of course, I have," Leo said. "The only reason I fell was because of my traitorous brother. And now that he's gone, I can finally assume my rightful place."

My teeth ground against each other. What right did this piece of shit have to talk about Gabriel like that?

I darted to him, the blade swinging in the air towards Leo. But all I clashed with was a string of light.

That gave Leo the chance to pull back. I could've gotten a hit in, but Aaron stopped me.

I twisted toward him to lecture him before he said, "What are You still doing here? Did You already forget about Anacora?"

Anacora. Of course, I hadn't forgotten. But did he really expect me to leave him with Leo?

"But—"

Aaron's eyes stabbed through me. "You better get out of my way."

I recognized that maniacal, icy tone. He could match Leo in strength now, but I still couldn't abandon him.

"Aaron," Heather spoke. "Please, let me fight with you."

"Me too," Ethan added.

Nathan brought his fists up. "All of us will fight with you."

"Hell, yeah!" Theo said.

"No. All of you are dead weight."

Heather's nostrils flared in offense. "We aren't—"

Leo sprinted at Aaron and kicked at his side, but Aaron blocked the blow with his bruised elbow. "*He's mine!*" Aaron screamed.

Light flashed before whips appeared around him. Not again. We raced out of range of Aaron's barrage, but stopped close-by and kept our eyes on the fight.

The ground rumbled from each hit of Aaron's whips. The

harsh light zipping through the air starkly contrasted the darkness around us.

"We're not leaving him," Heather told us.

The rest of them nodded, but I couldn't abandon them, too. "But with all this noise, the Pugnare will come rushing. You'll be crushed," I said.

"*Please.*" Theo waved his hand. "We've already been through the hardest thing an angel can go through. Let them come."

Indecision crushed my heart. I would never forgive myself if they died because I ran. But I couldn't let this chance to save Naomi pass by. What was the right thing to do? How would I—

Naomi's honey filled eyes encompassed my being. Her black, wavy hair smelled like grass from the fields. The softness of her chestnut skin was unmistakable.

I looked to the city.

Naomi was being held in the city.

Not another thought passed through my mind as I sprinted toward it, her call guiding me. "Bring her back!" Nathan yelled, pushing me farther.

THIRTY-THREE

THE GRASS UNDER MY FEET HARDENED INTO STONE. Buildings stacked around me, but the tallest one stood in the center of the city—the Gods' Palace.

But I wasn't being pulled to the center of the city like I'd expected. The connection dragged me through the alleyways, and I happily let it. *Right. Left. Left. Right. Left.*

Shouting echoed from the skies. I stopped beside a wall and looked up. Armored angels flew out of the city, toward the forest. I gulped down my apprehension and kept going, sticking to the walls of the buildings. Luckily, they didn't pay close attention to what was happening below them.

A smile grew on my lips as I got closer. The bell tower attached to the library. That was where she was.

I skidded to a stop in front of the looming door to slam it open. "NAOMI!"

No one was there. I focused on her presence, but there was nothing, like she had disappeared. But that couldn't be right. No one could just disappear.

I held the curved blade in front of me as I trailed my way up the spiraling staircase. The wood creaked and groaned under my feet.

A doorway opened to the second floor, and I stopped, peering in. The bookshelves and tables in the library were set up exactly like I remembered. But instead of seeing groups bundled together happily reading books, the room was eerily empty.

Naomi was the first one who'd shown me the library. Being cramped inside a room reading books never sounded appealing to me. Not until she sat next to me.

I tightened my grip on the handle and climbed higher. *She has to be here.*

When I reached the third and final floor, the enormous gold bell reflected my face on its side. I analyzed my reflection—my scruffy clothes and ragged appearance. My once nonexistent beard had grown longer, but that didn't matter.

I walked around the bell.

"Naomi?" I called out. "Naomi, where are you?"

There was no one on the other side. Just a door. The meditation room. I'd never been inside it, so I had no idea what to expect, but I grabbed the door handle and swung it open without a second thought.

I only took one step inside before my breathing stalled. A man with ivory skin stared at me from across the room. He wore gigantic golden armor with a sword hanging at His side. His straight black hair was compressed into a bun. The golden shade of His eyes matched His armor perfectly.

Anacora.

Neither of us moved. He didn't scowl or grimace or draw His sword, but intimidation pulsated from Him like shockwaves.

I squeezed the handle. "Where is Naomi?"

His expression remained unreadable. "You'll see her soon."

"What are You talking about?"

The floor exploded in front of me. I shielded my eyes. When

the dust settled, I lowered my arms. Inches from my face, a woman grabbed my wrists in the middle of a leap. A woman with light brown eyes.

Naomi.

We hit the open door and landed on the ground, my sword dropping out of reach. My head pounded from the impact, and my back was completely numb, but those were worthless concerns. The woman I'd been searching for all this time was right on top of me. Her warm brown skin and beautiful eyes hadn't changed at all.

I didn't have any words. All I wanted to do was wrap my arms around her and—

She punched my stomach. I spat up blood. The iron in my lungs choked my senses. How was she this strong?

Her palm squished my face. She tightened her grip and crushed my nose until I couldn't breathe.

I bumped my hip up and flipped over her with a long-lost reflex. Air rushed into my lungs. Before I could process what happened, I examined her below me.

That beautiful honey shade of brown her irises held was covered with a glass-like glaze.

Naomi took a swing at me. I caught her wrists and held her down. She struggled aimlessly, like a wild animal.

"Naomi. It's me!" If Anacora controlled her mind, she could hear me. I knew from experience. "I'm right here."

Her knee punched my groin. The color drained from my face as painful cramps echoed throughout my nether region. My breaths turned shallow as I tried recuperating. Apparently, even Gods couldn't handle getting hit in the balls.

She tossed me into the air. I instinctively covered my head as I crashed through the floor.

I hit the floor of the library below, the air knocked out of my lungs. Shards of wood stabbed my arms, but I had to *get up*.

I forced my feet to stand. My head buzzed. Blood trailed down my arms.

How long had He had her like this? To make her fight like some kind of a puppet was utterly cruel.

She dived through the hole she created. A bow and arrow of light formed in her arms midair. She let go and the arrow whizzed toward me.

I dodged. The wind from the arrow slapped me in the face. I watched it hit the table behind me and fling splinters into the air.

"Do you remember this place?" I asked.

She landed, bent her knees, and shot toward me. Her bow transformed into a sword. I ducked it easily. A bang affirmed that she hit something behind me.

"I remember when you dragged me here." I smiled despite the danger. "I tried to act excited, but my acting was terrible."

A throbbing pain plowed through my ribcage. When I looked down, I saw her sword of light. Blood soaked my chest where she'd stabbed me in the back. I should've kept my guard up, but my sluggish emotions controlled me.

A wave of coughs hit me. More blood. A familiar metallic taste filled my mouth. Every time I fought, I had tasted blood. Perhaps that was a sign that I was never meant to be on the battlefield.

Her breaths caressed the back of my neck. She could hear me. I knew she could.

"But when we got here..." The room spun. I was bleeding out. Already. *So pathetic.* "You picked... out a book for me... and we... we sat together in a corner... and I..."

I spit out more blood. My words escaped from me, just like my breaths. What I said next was nothing more than an intelligible mumble, but what I meant to say with complete sincerity was, *"I fell in love with you."*

Her sword of light faded away.

I tumbled to the floor. Each heartbeat pumped the blood out of my body. The pattern that made me weaker every second turned hypnotic, but I had so much more to say and do. I had to protect her.

My hands wavered by my chest where my blood spouted. I tried channeling the energy into my wound, but it wouldn't work. Why wasn't it working?

Anacora landed on the floor with His wings stretched out and walked toward me.

I couldn't pass out now. I had to save her. But how? My muscles wouldn't move. I could barely keep my eyes open.

The strength I thought I possessed as a God... it was gone. Maybe it wasn't true to begin with. Maybe Aaron was mistaken. There was no way I could be the Great Healer if I was this weak.

Anacora stopped. I saw His lips move, and I heard noises coming from His mouth, but the words themselves escaped me.

My eyes shut. *It's over now.*

The pain faded into numbness. All I could do was listen to the footsteps of someone nearby. Probably Anacora, or Naomi. *Naomi, I'm too weak to help you.*

"Naomi?"

That voice forced my eyes to open again. Why was he here? What was he thinking?

Nathan stood in the doorway. His side burned from a fierce blow he'd received earlier. His umber eyes trembled at the sight of his sister.

I tried to tell him to run, but a burst of pain made me writhe instead.

"Anilin," Anacora said. "Stay out of this."

Yes. "N... Nathan..." He had to run. "Go." For some reason, Anacora was fixated on having me fighting Naomi. After all, He didn't attack Nathan on sight. Nathan could still run.

Nathan's body shook, like his breath. His gaze traveled from me, and back to Naomi. He stare lingered on his sister for much longer, though. "What did You do to them?"

Damn it. Of course, Nathan wouldn't run. Naomi was the sister he'd been looking for, for years.

I curled my arms, putting my hands to my chest and summoning the light. *Heal, dammit.* She needed me to heal. Both of them did.

The light sparked in my hands and poured into my wound. Thank goodness. Hopefully, it stayed that way. Failing powers were not what I needed right now.

I was able to stand on my knees as Nathan charged at Anacora with a wrath-filled cry.

"No!"

My feet pushed off the ground. I reached out. The tip of my finger grazed Nathan's shirt as Anacora spoke. "If you won't stay out of this, then you'll be a part of it, too."

Nathan jumped back, leaving me flinging full-speed towards a wall. I skid across the floor to stop myself. Luckily, by the time I reached the wall, my nose barely pressed against it. If I'd put on the brakes any later, I probably would've smashed right through it.

I flipped around.

Nathan stood a couple paces away from Anacora, farther than before. Good. He didn't attack Him.

Nathan's eyes locked onto Naomi's. She stared back at him. Instead of sharing Nathan's reaction, she simply stood there. No expression, no trembling, just silence.

"Nathan. Go back and tell the others that I'm dealing with Anacora. I'll save her. I promise," I said while Anacora let me.

Nathan didn't respond. He analyzed Naomi. The terror reflected in his eyes had been replaced with a blank, unfeeling look.

Anacora's words crashed into me. *If you won't stay out of this, then you'll be a part of it, too.*

My heart spiked.

Nathan darted towards her. Blades of light flashed in Naomi's hands. Nathan's fists glowed.

I sprinted after him.

Naomi swung her knife at Nathan. I gripped her wrist, stopping her before she slashed him. I flipped back to Nathan and swept his leg. He tumbled onto the ground.

Something jabbed my side. Naomi's free blade dug into me. A strained breath seeped from my mouth as I forced the pain out of my mind.

Nathan stood and dashed around me, to Naomi. Anacora was making Nathan attack Naomi. Why? Was having me battle her not enough?

I snatched Naomi's hand that still buried her dagger in me as light bloomed in Nathan's palm. Hopefully my grip on her would hold. I zipped and zagged across the room when Nathan fired his laser, keeping my hold on Naomi.

"Nathan, you have to fight it!" Shouting might've been pointless, but it didn't stop me.

Naomi bit my shoulder. I winced, but I had to keep moving. I jumped high into the air. Nathan's laser followed me closer than before, but I couldn't let him hurt her.

I eyed Anacora, who did nothing. He was forcing innocent siblings to fight to the death while He watched. That was something only the worst, most sadistic tyrants would do. How could He do this to His own angels?

His indifferent expression turned into a sneer. "Never mind," He told Nathan. "Just kill yourself."

Those words froze time itself. He said them as if Nathan's very existence was a nuisance, but Nathan didn't deserve that. He didn't deserve to die like that.

Nathan stopped firing. I landed on the ground. I wouldn't let him die.

I yanked Naomi's blade from my side and shot towards Nathan, her teeth finally releasing me as I did. Nathan formed his own knife of light and held it firmly in his hands.

He was going to live.

He raised his knife to his throat when I snatched his hands. I squeezed his palms, forcing them down to the floor. Nathan slowly extended the blade. At this rate, the blade would reach his neck.

I had to knock him out, but I wasn't used to my strength yet. What if I accidentally hurt him, or killed him?

Anacora charged toward us, and was beside us in mere moments. He lunged His sword at Nathan. Ancrora was about to kill Nathan Himself.

I instinctively shot my free hand toward His blade, but what was I supposed to do? What could I do?

Sparks clanged as steel clashed against steel.

My mouth dropped when I saw something in my hand—a double-ended sword with wide, angled blades and a wrapped staff-like handle.

Anacora jumped back with calculating eyes. There was no doubt that He recognized it, too.

It was the Galactica. The same sword Aaron had stolen before he fell, and the same one mentioned in the legend of the Great Healer. Of me. Where the hell had it come from? And how was such a big weapon so light?

"Caleb?" Nathan mumbled. The knife of light in his hands had disappeared. "What... what happened?"

Nathan was back to normal? Did it have something to do with the Galactica? Whatever the answers, I didn't have the time to find them.

I dropped his hands. "We found her. Keep her occupied while I deal with Him."

He shook, taking it in all over again, before he steadied. "Okay."

Anacora frowned, pointing His steel at me. "You should concentrate on Your new opponent. But I suppose a healer wouldn't know that."

He wanted to fight me Himself now? But why did He change His mind? The answer was on the back of my tongue, but the adrenaline made it hard to think.

I widened my stance and held the sword close to me. Even if He was right, I had to try. I couldn't begin to imagine what He had put Naomi through; how long He had her under His control while I was doing nothing, stuck in that backwater town with Todd getting drunk every night. Starting now, I had to make it up to her.

Nathan charged toward his sister before Anacora appeared in front of me. He aimed for my stomach. I blocked His strike with my blade. My feet slid on the floor as He pushed me back.

His sword aimed at my head. I managed another block when something fell to the floor. Anacora crouched on the ground next to my hand. He cut off my hand. Fiery pain shot up my arm as white blood puddled onto the wood. *White blood.* I swallowed a scream, but a gargled sound came out.

"I *did* tell You to pay attention." He skipped across the room. The ceiling, the table, the floor. My eyes couldn't track Him with His speed. Was He holding back earlier? But how was He moving faster than another God could see?

Cuts lacerated my body. My arms, legs, back, and stomach. I waved the sword around, but not a single hit landed. And none of my injuries would heal. Why wouldn't they heal?

His blade dug deep into my shoulder. The pain forced my grip open, and the sword dropped to the ground.

He was right. *That sword is useless.*

"You should be proud." He shoved His sword in deeper. "You put up a great fight for a healer."

A dagger of light emerged near my throat. But it wasn't from His hand. I recognized that hand.

Naomi won. She had beaten Nathan, and she was about to cut my throat. With Anacora backing off, I could differentiate between my pain and Nathan's. He had been stabbed like me. If I had just swallowed my pride and forced them to go back when they snuck in through the portal, none of them would be here.

Anacora smirked cruelly before He pulled his sword out of my shoulder. White blood glistened on the steal. *My* blood.

He stepped aside to reveal Nathan. He resembled a pin cushion, blood seeping from his many stab wounds.

Why was it that everywhere I went, people ended up bleeding?

Naomi walked in front of me, streaks of scarlet on her cheeks.

"Your rescuer is gone, and You'll be killed by Your own soulmate," Anacora said. "What a tragic end."

Why? He could've killed me already. We were in combat moments ago. He was insane. Still, as I looked at Naomi's face and her succulent lips, a strange emotion burned inside me.

Naomi leaned in closer. Her breath wisped against my chin. She was so close to me, and her hair looked so soft. My lips parted into a smile.

She slit my throat. The dagger in her hand faded away. I stepped back.

Despite what should've happened, I felt nothing. Nothing except a new rush of strength, drenched in familiarity.

My sword flew into my hand. I drew in a sharp, adrenaline-filled breath. How the hell was I alive?

Naomi drew her fist back. I thrust my sword. She hit the ground.

I gasped. What the hell did I do? My muscles had moved without thinking, but I didn't feel any pain from her or see any blood. I had stopped before the steel pierced her. Hopefully she could forgive me, for whatever the fuck I just did.

My sword beamed with a golden light. I had no idea what it

meant, but I pointed it at Anacora with my remaining hand and scowled. This fight had only just begun.

He glared back at me and anchored the handle of His sword by His head. "Why can't You just die?"

The reason was His indulgence. If He had just taken this fight seriously from the start, I most likely would've been killed. But He didn't. He approached this fight like some messed up science experiment.

My left wrist burned where my hand used to be, and the pain from my shoulder burrowed deep into my chest. The bleeding had stopped, but the pain remained. I couldn't let it stop me.

He swung at me. I jumped back, but He lunged forward. I pushed His sword away.

He whirled His blade to my side. When I parried the strike, I shot across the room. Shards of glass pierced me as I smashed through the window.

I still wasn't strong enough, but giving up wasn't an option. Stabbing my sword into the wall, I stopped my descent, my shoulder throbbing as I squeezed the handle.

Anacora dived from the window, His sword aimed at me. I swung my sword from the wall and blocked. We fell together.

Shit.

We smashed onto the road. Bricks blasted through the air as the buildings around us were destroyed.

Anacora towered over me and pushed His sword toward my chest. The handle of my sword was the only thing stopping it. My arm struggled under Him. I shoved my handless arm on my blade, but His blade still inched down.

The bell tower. Nathan and Naomi were still inside the building, and it was mere wreckage now. Every brick and stone fell on top of them. Fuck.

"I underestimated You," He remarked.

The muscles in my arms burned. My wrists touched my chest. I had to push harder.

He shoved His sword deeper. A loud crack rang in my ears. I let out a blood-curdling scream.

My arms loosened, desperately wanting to drop to my sides, but I had to keep pushing. All He was doing was pushing into my pommel. From that alone, He cracked the bones in my ribcage.

He thrust the blade deeper and my arms finally caved in and dropped. My scream silenced in my throat, but the agony still ran deep. I took shallow breaths, but even that wasn't enough to stop it. Each breath made the stinging pain worse.

He stood up and kicked my sword away. An excited grin painted His face as Anacora raised His sword for the final strike.

I had to move, but my body wouldn't obey me. He swung His blade.

Memories of my life dashed across my mind. Meeting Naomi, getting rescued by Aaron, seeing Gabriel's decapitated head. All of it was for nothing.

Suddenly, a pair of hazel eyes I couldn't place appeared along with a soft, male voice. *"If you ever need me, just hold up this sword. I will always find you."*

The sword.

I reached for my sword. The tip of my fingers barely touched the woven, metallic handle. My chest ached relentlessly as my arm stretched out.

Sharp pain radiated across my body. I glanced back. His blade punched through my chest. Pure white seeped from my wound, but I still lived. He wanted to torture me more. I could use that to my advantage.

I gritted my teeth and reached farther. My vision doubled. The world spun under me as I breathed in fiery iron.

Some of my fingers wrapped around the handle. I dragged the

sword closer and gripped it as hard as I could. But could I even lift it anymore?

I couldn't question it. There were no other options.

My arm wobbled as I tried hoisting up the sword. My mangled shoulder screamed in protest.

The sword had felt lighter than air moments ago. Now, my strength was escaping me. Still, I had to keep pushing. There were too many people that depended on me.

I summoned all my willpower to inch the handle into the air. Every part of me shook from the torture of my numerous injuries, but I didn't stop.

Anacora removed His sword.

Higher.

He slammed His blade through my arm. A hot flash of pain came with it. I gnashed my teeth and raised the sword higher, using my elbow as a prop.

The cut widened as I moved. The pain clawed deeper until my sword was about a foot above the air. *That should be high enough.*

I grinned, looking at Anacora confidently for the first time. His desire to drag out my death would be His downfall.

His head jerked back in surprise.

"You're." I winced. "Finished."

A bright light exploded from my steel, forcing my eyes shut. I slowly opened my eyes again and stared in complete awe at what I saw. Her blond hair and elegant dress danced in the breeze.

Lady Elisha. She was here, and Her body wasn't made of light like before. She was corporeal.

Anacora dropped His sword on the ground with a clang. "It can't be."

Soldiers flew overhead. Each one of them froze and gawked at Her. Some of them spoke. Although I had no idea what they said, it was easy to figure out what, or rather who, they were talking about.

I knew the sword would summon someone, but I didn't expect it to be Her of all people. She was dead. This was impossible.

Elisha looked at Anacora. "I knew Your ambition would get ahead of You, and I'm sorry I couldn't do anything about it sooner."

"You mean *Our* ambition," He said with a frown. "I am Your reincarnation." His fist hit his chest. "You always had it inside You. You just didn't use it right."

There was a moment of shameful silence. "I know." She took a step closer.

He picked up His sword and slid into a fighting stance. "Not another step."

She froze and everyone followed suit. The only confirmation I had that this moment existed was the extreme pain that coursed through me.

"Caleb." My heart fluttered at Her calling my name. "When I'm gone, You must stay here. Anacora won't reincarnate until He dies, so someone else must lead in the meantime. I can only hope that the angels here will accept You."

Anacora said something but I blocked out His voice out as She looked over Her shoulder at me. Tears glistened in Her eyes. A sad smile painted Her lips.

"I love You."

Pools of tears ran from my eyes. Tears that I didn't know I would shed.

My tears clouded my vision as Anacora charged at Her. All I saw was a silver blade stabbing through Her throat.

I choked. I wanted to scream, but my wounds silenced me. Elisha grabbed the steel and She squeezed His shoulder with Her other hand.

"What are you doing?" Anacora's eyes flared with anger before

Their bodies turned into a bright light. I squinted to see the light crash back into my sword.

They were gone.

My head thumped to the ground. A sense of bitter relief washed over me. After all that fighting, She got rid of Him so easily.

The angels above me argued amongst themselves.

"Did They just go inside the sword?"

"But wasn't it hidden? How did *he* get it?"

"That doesn't matter now. Anacora's gone. Lady Elisha betrayed Him!"

"No. He betrayed Her when He stabbed Her. You saw it yourself."

"You're right."

"It can't be."

Their words swarmed around like bees until the letters jumbled into an unrecognizable mess.

Naomi. I glanced at the bell tower that was now mere wreckage. I saw her, unconscious and crushed under the debris.

My body trembled. I had to get up. She needed me. This wasn't over yet.

I dropped my sword and swung, rather wobbly, onto my stomach. I crawled out of the crater Anacora had created, using my sore arms to push myself forward. Cold numbness pumped through my body, but as long as I could move, I'd keep going. My arms inched me closer. But they still looked so far from me, no matter how far I crawled.

I extended my arms again, but I couldn't pull them back. My muscles wouldn't obey me. The sides of my vision turned white as the wreckage softened into gray and brown blurs. My strength that had held out for so long finally crumbled.

CHAPTER

THIRTY-FOUR

I LOOKED OUT ONTO THE LUSCIOUS, ROLLING HILLS. KIDS chased each other and flew around playfully, trying to catch one another. I watched their game blissfully.

"I knew I'd find You here."

I glanced over My shoulder.

My brother leaned onto a pillar of Our house. The skin under His brown eyes dotted with green creased from a smile.

"Weren't You going to spar with someone?" I asked. "What are You up to?"

"Nothing."

I stared at Him as He looked away guiltily. He wore His loose sparring clothes. The blue color had faded away over the years. And His arms were hidden behind Him.

I stood up and stepped closer. "That's not very convincing."

He chuckled. "You know I'm not a good liar."

My arms folded over my chest. I hated when He acted this childish.

"I made something for You."

He did? There wasn't anything I really wanted. He never asked if I wanted anything, either. Jerk.

He swung his arms out in front of Him. A sword stretched out on His palms, but it didn't look like any sword I'd ever seen.

It was double-bladed with unusually wide, diagonally cut blades. The handle had been tightly wrapped with metal.

My confusion increased. "You made Me a sword?" If I could even call it that.

"Yes."

I waved my hand in front of Me. "But you know I can't. I—"

"Yes, You can." His voice was steady, serious. "Please, just hold it."

A sword.

My whole life, each time I tried to fight, it backfired. Even thinking about it made Me sick. But disputes couldn't always be solved with words alone. My brother dealt with squabbles amongst the angels while I did nothing.

I reached out my hand and grabbed the pommel. The handle shocked Me with cold as I picked it up. Contradicting its large size, I held it easily with one hand.

My eyes widened when a presence appeared. Energy swam around the sword. It connected to My energy with a mind of its own.

My brother gave Me a knowing smirk.

I tapped the steel with My free hand. "How did You do this?"

"I mixed it with some of My energy." He wrapped His arm over My shoulders and admired His work. "It's able to absorb energy from angels so You can use it to fight."

"Really?"

"Yeah. And You can heal with it, too." He rocked his hand from side to side. "Although, sapping away too much energy might make them pass out," He added guiltily.

A grin split My lips despite that warning.

"Do You like it?"

Without a word, I hugged Him. He laughed like the jerk He was. His arms eventually hugged Me back.

With this, I could help Him and all of Our creations. I could keep them safe. Finally.

∾

RAIN SLAPPED MY FACE.

I lay on the muddy ground. White blood drained from My body. Each breath became shallower as I crawled closer to death.

Black blood and dirt drenched My sword. The demons had been defeated, but so had I.

My heavy eyes gave out and closed. When My brother's hazel eyes appeared in my mind, a tiny smile formed on My lips. Then, everything turned black for the last time. Or so I thought.

∾

MY EYES BLINKED OPEN.

I studied the stone ceiling above Me. Sunlight peeked through a giant hole beside Me, and I lay in bed. What was left of My shirt after My battle was gone, but My wounds had been wrapped with bandages.

The man in My dream. He was My brother. My brother was the man with hazel eyes.

I remembered Him. I remembered everything. I had died defeating the last of the demons, and had reincarnated many, many years later. The damage must've been great with such a long recovery period.

To think I died a fighter. It was ironic.

And the reason I couldn't heal in the fight against Anacora the first time was because I was subconsciously trying to summon the sword. That was one of the kinks *I* discovered. But the second quirk was well-known by My brother when He made it: I wasn't able to heal Myself when using My sword to heal another, and I had been subconsciously healing Nathan. That must've been what I was doing. But after I'd found that drawback, there was nothing I found to fix it. Any weapon had its drawbacks, even the good ones.

Someone's pain echoed nearby. Ethan leaned on the wall next to the doorway. "You're awake."

Blood peppered his calf and his head.

"Is everyone okay?" I asked.

He edged his way over to My bed. "Everyone's alive. Aaron got hurt really bad, but as soon as we have charged-up healers, he'll be okay."

I sighed. I thought I wouldn't see Aaron again after Leo found us in the forest, but he was alive after all.

"He saved our lives out there," he continued with a thoughtful look on his face. "I just wish... there wasn't so much death."

I frowned. "The Pugnare soldiers?"

Ethan nodded. "We tried to keep it to a minimum, but that doesn't always happen, I suppose."

A bittersweet feeling overcame Me. Still, at the very least, the Swans had lived.

"What about Naomi?"

His eyes darkened. "Her head and her arm got hit pretty badly, but she woke up a while ago and attacked us. We had to chain her up. She hasn't moved since."

Damn it. Even though He was sealed inside the sword, Anacora still retained His influence over her. Hopefully, He hadn't done the same with Me.

I grabbed the frame of the bed and forced Myself up. My chest stung. The only time I felt this persistent pain was...

Ethan stuck out his hands. "No. You shouldn't move until someone can heal You. Lie back down."

I stood up anyway. The stiffness of My wounds made it hard to walk, but I moved forward.

Whatever demented method Anacora had experimented with, I had to see her. That was My top priority.

Ethan swooped his arm under mine. "At least let me help You."

I nodded. "Thanks."

We trailed along a hallway outlined with empty rooms. Holes had been dug through the walls, but not enough to make the building come crashing down, apparently.

When Anacora demolished the bell tower and everything fell on top of her, all I managed to do was raise My sword. There was so much more I had to do.

My head shot up. Our connection tightened. She was right around the corner. I rushed ahead, shrugging off Ethan's arm. He chased after Me.

"Wait. Don't run!"

I turned into the room. Heather jumped onto her feet when she saw Me. Theo asked Me something, but I couldn't hear him. Or rather, I didn't bother listening.

Naomi was there. She sat in front of a gigantic rock, chains wrapping her body. Nathan talked to her from a low crouch. He stopped for a moment to look at Me. The hope in his eyes was crumbling. Still, he gazed at his sister again and kept trying.

"Do you remember me?"

No response.

"I'm your brother. My name's Nathan now, but you'll remember me as Anilin."

Nothing.

He smiled. "It's okay if you don't remember me. It's been at least fifty years since I've seen you." He glanced at the floor. "I've been trying to find you ever since."

I closely studied her face. The blood on her cheeks—Nathan's blood—had long dried. Her wavy, black hair had been tangled from battle. And there wasn't a single hint of an expression on her face. Not even a flinch.

Nathan bit his lip and stared at the ground.

I had to fix this. With resurfacing confidence, I stepped around Nathan and in front of her.

"Don't get too close," Ethan warned. "That's when she attacked us."

I sat down in front of her. The chains snapped. Her arms lunged toward Me as she screeched a battle cry.

"Caleb!" Heather shouted.

I pulled her in close. My hand grabbed the back of her head. I shot every ounce of strength into My palm.

GOLDEN LIGHT STRETCHED FOR MILES. I searched aimlessly for her, but she wasn't anywhere in sight.

"Naomi!"

I circled in place. Her mind was so empty.

"NAOMI!"

I looked around, but all I saw was a bright, infinite abyss. But that was impossible. Anacora would be here if He was controlling her, and this was her mind, so she *had* to be here.

"Caleb?" a voice spoke behind Me.

I gasped. Tears dotted My eyes. I took in a slow, deep breath as I turned around.

Naomi's light brown eyes twinkled. Her black hair was messy from battle. Blood dripped from her scarlet hands, staining her mind-scape red. But her eyes. He could never take the beauty from her eyes.

Her hand hesitantly rose and touched My cheek. She rubbed her palm against My sweaty beard.

"Is it really you?"

I swallowed down more tears. "Yeah." I nodded. "It's really Me."

She laughed. And another voice copied her's.

I swung around, gripping her hand. But there was no one in sight. Still, goosebumps crawled and skittered across My skin. Someone was definitely watching us. It could only be one person — Anacora.

"Caleb. You have to leave," Naomi ordered.

"I'm not leaving without you," I said, still scanning the area.

She took a concern-filled breath out. "*Caleb.*"

A shadow whipped toward Me. I parried its strike. The dark blur faded.

Naomi slid out of my grip and leaned against My back. "Then let me fight with you."

I couldn't object before it pounced onto My side.

The shadow jabbed and kicked and clawed. It circled around us. We blocked and parried. The light pulled Me, quickening after each hit.

"CALEB!" she shouted.

I gasped. Naomi was sinking. She was waist down already.

"Naomi!" I clasped onto her outreached hand. Not before My back seared from a raging pain. I couldn't hold back My wrangled scream, but I wouldn't let go so easily. Not when I was so close.

Naomi's eyes bulged in terror, but her expression quickly changed. Her other palm shot out and flashed, just like a flashlight. The light reached everywhere, until I could barely see.

"Leave him *alone!*"

Then, there was nothing. No pain, no looming eyes. Just light. And her.

That golden hue of Naomi's mind-scape was gone, replaced with a pure, white light. Now, Anacora was gone for good. I didn't like what that burning sensation reminded Me of when I got hit, but she was well worth it.

"Caleb." She held My hands. "I'm so happy to see you."

I didn't know what to say back. I mean, I had plenty of things to say, but none of them seemed good enough. Not with Him finally gone. Not with her in front of Me. And so close.

My lips pounced onto hers. Her silky-smooth lips pushed back. I breathed every ounce of her in. She didn't smell as sweetly as before, but it was still *her* scent. My fingers ran through her tangled hair. Her hand gently touched My chest.

WE PULLED AWAY from each other as our surroundings slowly returned. She breathed into My ear, "I could barely recognize you with that beard."

I laughed. Even after all this time and the ordeal we'd just went through, she still liked teasing Me.

"Naomi?"

She looked up to whomever called her name. Nathan gently held her shoulder. I stood up and backed away, giving the siblings a moment.

Naomi squinted her eyes. "*Anilin?*"

Nathan grinned as tears built up in his eyes. He tackled her to the ground and squeezed her. She giggled and hugged him back.

"I missed you," Nathan wailed.

"I missed you, too."

We'd finally found her. After all this time, Naomi was here with us. My wide grin wouldn't fade. I could've smiled like this for the rest of eternity.

"All right." She patted his back. "Get off of me so I can breathe."

Nathan hesitantly stood up and put out his hand. His nervous smile showed his embarrassment. She took it and hoisted herself up.

Her grin turned into a pondering stare as she studied her brother. From his messy wavy, black hair that they shared to his height.

"You've grown so much."

He nodded without a word, but his eyes sparkled.

Naomi's smile resurfaced until she noticed My bandaged left arm. "Caleb..." Her lips quivered as she walked toward Me and gently grabbed where My hand used to be. "Your hand... What—"

"It's okay." I stroked My remaining hand through her tangled hair. "We're together again. That's all that matters."

Tears gathered in her eyes before an exasperated laugh escaped from her. I could've spent all day with her now that she was right in front of Me, but I had a job to do first.

"What exactly is Aaron's condition?" I asked them.

"Aaron is still unconscious." Heather's brows creased her nose. "I tried to heal him, but most of my energy was spent during the fight. Everyone's was."

I bowed My head. "Tell Me where My sword is, and I can heal everyone."

Heather flinched before composing herself.

I would've summoned it Myself, but these injuries I received were more severe than usual, even if My opponent was another God. It would've been easier for her to take Me to it.

Naomi's brows tilted. "What are you talking about, Caleb?"

Right. She didn't know anything. Not yet. "I'll tell you later."

She grabbed her wrists nervously like she did when we were kids and nodded.

"It's not far from here." Heather stepped in front of Me. "I'll show You where it is." Then she walked out.

Naomi appeared beside Me. I wrapped My arm around her waist and followed Heather with everyone else trailing behind.

My sword couldn't be far.

~

WE WALKED in the city streets. Armored angels ogled Me and whispered amongst themselves, but none of them moved to stop Me. After what they saw, I understood their confusion well. But calming their concerns would have to wait.

The familiar energy of the sword connected to Me. My sword lay in the shallow crater in the road where I had last used it.

Heather gestured to it with her hand. "There it is."

Naomi let go of Me as I walked toward it. I passed Heather and stepped down where the blade laid. A bittersweet feeling overcame Me.

When My brother connected His own energy to it, He ensured that He would be sealed inside when He died, and every one of His reincarnations followed Him. That was probably intentional, knowing Him. Still, I didn't know one of Them could be sealed inside while alive. The seal probably wouldn't hold Anacora for long, but that wasn't the priority right now.

I picked it up with My remaining hand and held it in front of Me. Light wisped around the shining metal as I drew out the power stored within it. Then the light shot out towards the injured. The surrounding angels gasped as the radiance passed through them and closed their bloodied wounds.

"Holy shit," Theo said.

Ethan, Nathan, and Heather marveled at the healed angels around them as well as their own mended bodies. Even the Pugnare marveled at My work. But some of them hovered over bodies of their fellow angels, wailing. I cringed at the sight. Even with all of My healing abilities, I couldn't bring back the dead.

Naomi stared at Me with confused eyes. Her frightened

expression was a sore thumb among the grins surrounding us. "Caleb?"

I walked to her, My sword in My grasp. Her eyes locked onto Mine. Each line of her honey-brown irises stood out to Me.

"A-are... Are you Him?"

I gave a slow nod.

Her eyebrows sank. "Why didn't You tell me?"

I glanced at the sword reflexively. "I didn't know Myself until recently." My gaze returned to her. "I'm sorry that I—"

"I should've known. I should've known from how remarkable Your healing was." Her eyes smiled, even though her lips barely moved. "You don't have to apologize for anything."

Without another word, I leaned into her lips. She kissed Me back. I wanted to dig deeper into her skin, but now wasn't the time or the place. I pulled Myself away and looked at the scene behind us.

"He used the sword," an armored angel said.

They murmured and whispered things about Me. A presence I recognized approached Me from behind, drowning out their words. I swung behind Me.

"Caleb!" Leo shouted, stalking toward Me with that familiar scowl wrinkling his face.

I bent My knees and held My sword steadfast. Leo was the strongest angel alive, but I would beat him if I had to.

Before any strikes were dealt, he dropped onto his knees before Me. I lowered My sword slightly, but I wouldn't let My guard down so easily.

"I'm sorry. I didn't know You were the Great Healer." He bowed until his head touched the ground. "I don't deserve my wings." His wings popped out of his back with swift finesse. "I'm ready for my punishment."

Sharp exhales and gossip exploded around Me.

My arm lowered the sword to My side. Leo was always loyal to

Me and My brother, but so was Gabriel. Gabriel was dead because of him, his own brother.

I swung My blade no more than an inch from the stem of his feathered wings.

What would Gabriel want Me to do? What would My *brother* want Me to do?

I scowled as My sword fell back to My side. "*Get up.*"

He stood without a word. His chin rose in preparation for what he probably thought was about to happen.

"Gather up the Pugnare. Inform those that didn't see what happened."

His eyes widened. "But—"

"That's an order from your God."

He bit his lip as the gears turned in his head. He eventually nodded and turned around, taking off into the sky.

I didn't know what My brother or Gabriel would want Me to do, but it didn't seem right to kill him. Leo was nothing more than a loyal soldier, even if imagining Gabriel's severed head boiled My blood.

I faced the crowd.

"He's the Great Healer?" someone said.

"But how?" another one added.

I steadied Myself with a deep breath. They needed a leader now more than ever.

CHAPTER

THIRTY-FIVE

I LAY IN THE BIGGEST BED I HAD EVER SEEN. NAOMI'S HEAD rested on My chest. My hand mindlessly combed through her soft, wavy hair.

We were in My chamber at the palace. Despite the slightly familiar design of the golden walls and the open windows, it was strange. It didn't feel like Mine.

"Caleb." Her leg wrapped around Mine. "I missed You."

"I missed you, too."

I rested My chin on her head and breathed her in. At least, for now, all I could feel was bliss. She was safe in My arms, finally.

I closed My eyes as My thoughts drifted, a content smile clinging to My face. And as I was about to fall back asleep, she whispered, "We should get ready. Today's a big day."

My eyes opened. This smile on My face wouldn't go away. "You know, I *am* the Great Healer. I can reschedule anything I want." Even with how important this was, I didn't want to leave this bed with her in it.

She slapped My arm. "Caleb." The snark in her voice starkly contrasted her light-hearted laughter. "Don't say things like that."

"Okay, okay," I said as I sat up. She followed Me and got off the bed to get dressed. I tried not to get too distracted as I did the same.

She was right. Today was a big day—too big to reschedule.

~

I STOOD ON THE STAGE. Thousands upon thousands of angels looked up at Me.

Nathan stood in front of Me, his green robe lined with golden threads. He looked at Theo and tried to stifle his growing smile. Theo's fiery-red outfit complemented Nathan's perfectly.

"Thank you for coming, everyone." The murmurs in the crowd stopped. "I know that these are confusing times. It's only been a month since Anacora was defeated, and I know some of you are still suspicious of Me. But I'm glad that we can at least celebrate the union of these two souls."

The crowd cheered. Naomi's voice screamed the loudest. The shouts weren't traditional, but it felt right.

Nathan and Theo sat on the pillows in front of them with grace.

I followed them into a crouch. I touched their heads and took a moment to look at them. Theo didn't even try to hide his cocky grin. Nathan forced his lips down, but I knew he was just as excited.

My left wrist started to burn.

Not now.

I closed My eyes to ignore the pain and focus on them. It wasn't long before I felt their energies bubbling around them. I slowly pulled some out like strings of yarn.

I waved My arms in the air and connected the strings. I opened My eyes. A line of light connected them from their foreheads.

We stood up. They stared at each other in awe.

I grinned. "Your souls are now one. May your love last forever!"

Before the crowd could cheer, the lovers clutched each other. Nathan held Theo's cheek close as they kissed.

The crowd went wild. I almost joined in and clapped for them. Then I remembered. My left hand wasn't there anymore, but I couldn't let that stop this happy moment.

Nathan pulled away with a blushing face, but Theo couldn't stop grinning.

The string of light faded away, but the connection stayed forever. I finally made it up to Naomi's, no, *My* little brother.

CHAPTER

THIRTY-SIX

LADY ELISHA FLOATED PEACEFULLY IN THE WATER OF THE LAKE. Flowers adorned Her hair and Her hands. Angels surrounded the pool with mournful faces.

I stared at Her lifeless body, holding back my tears swelling in my throat. My palm strangled Naomi's hand tighter.

"Why did She have to die?" I whispered, my words only audible enough for Naomi to hear.

"She did it to protect us."

I knew that, but why did it have to be Her?

Her body glowed as the lake began to stir. Then Her corpse rose above the water and morphed into the figure of a child. She was gone for good now.

The new God lowered down to the lake. They touched the surface of the water with Their feet as the light faded.

Long, black hair dipped into the pool. His white clothes matched His porcelain skin. His golden eyes reminded me of Gabriel's, but something was different about them. Maybe they were a different hue?

"I am Anacora," He spoke. "I am your new God."

Everyone went onto their knees and bowed. The tears that I had been hiding managed to fall down my cheek. At least my face was hidden.

~

I FLEW in the sky and spotted the lake below Me. So many memories with contradicting feelings were at that lake that I didn't know what to feel anymore. If I had known My identity sooner, maybe I could've saved Elisha. Why didn't She tell Me?

"Caleb?"

Naomi appeared beside Me, gliding above the town. The only damage left was the crater Anacora and I made when We fell. Angels hurried around, hoisting the bases of buildings into place and hammering bricks into the walls. A few angels gently flew the new, shiny golden bell back into the reassembled bell tower.

Of course, a lot of the trees were destroyed in the forest, too. Light sparked into the ground as the healers worked to restore the woods.

I looked at Naomi and replaced My thoughtful frown with a smile. "What is it?"

She bit her lip. "Most of the city is restored, and angels are starting to adjust. Since a lot of them were under Lord Anacora's direct mind control, they're just relieved to have their lives back."

I nodded. Since the battle, Leo was a great help in convincing some of the more stubborn angels to accept the change. That wasn't surprising, considering it was well-known he wouldn't do anything not in the God's best interest. I'd tried forgiving him for killing his own brother, but it wasn't easy. In fact, I still hadn't forgiven him. My own guilt wouldn't be completely swallowed either. It was My fault Gabriel fell in the first place.

Without looking at her, I reached out My hand. She grasped it without a word. We flew over Heaven, together, as one.

EPILOGUE

Anacora's golden armor shone brilliantly in the endless white abyss. He gazed at the vast landscape in front of Him with a blank look on His face.

Elisha walked toward Him from behind and stopped. Even in the silence, She sensed the anger brewing from Him.

"Where did you put Me?" He asked, His voice devoid of emotion.

"We're inside the Galactica. We put Our soul in it long ago. Our reincarnations are pulled into it after They die."

His expression was a perfect mask—close to indifference—as He pondered His situation. Then a grin appeared. "Then it can only hold Me for so long. I'm not dead, and I'll soon be free."

Elisha scowled. "Maybe. But when that time comes, Our brother will finally kill You."

His grin faded as He realized the truth in Her words. This seal was incredibly strong. It would take at least a century to break free.

He chuckled. "Then I wonder why I still have my hold on him."

Elisha held in a gasp as a chill rippled over Her. "What do You mean?"

His heinous smile deepened. "And My experiments will soon be complete."

Acknowledgments

Thank you to Rebecca Jaycox of Book Butchers for tearing up this novel and making it the best it can be.

Also, thank you Jenna Moreci for your countless YouTube videos and writing advices. I know you'll probably never read this, but you've helped me improve immensely throughout my writing journey, so thank you.

Thank you to Chloe Humphries for drafting the book cover, and to the artists at Mibl Art for finishing her work. Both of you helped design the perfect wrapping for my story.

And thank you to all the beta readers that helped this story build to the published novel it is now. I am so grateful for all of your comments and not-so-sugar-coated advice.

ABOUT THE AUTHOR

Hi there! My name is Lillian McCoy. I'm an emerging fantasy author. This is my first novel, but I hope to publish many more.

For updates and more, check out my website:
www.lilliantmccoy.com/author-site

 x.com/LillianTMcCoy
instagram.com/lilliantmccoy_author